THUNDER
AND LIGHTNING

Book Three
in the
Keenan Chronicles

By Deborah I. Mahy

Illustrated by the author

To Taylor:
"Think" magic!
Deborah J. Mahy

April 03

iii

Canadian Cataloguing in Publication Data

Mahy, Deborah I. (Deborah Irene), 1967-
Thunder and Lightning
(Keenan chronicles; bk.3)

ISBN 0-9685340-3-1

I. Title. II. Series: Mahy, Deborah I. (Deborah Irene), 1967
Keenan chronicles; bk.3.

PS8576.A4815T47 2001   jC813'.54
C2001-902845-8   PZ7.M27729Th2001

Published by ASHLIN BOOKS
Hamilton, Ontario, Canada
Copyright 2001 Deborah I. Mahy

Also by ASHLIN BOOKS:
-Fire, Water, Earth and Air
-The Teacher's Guide to Fire, Water, Earth and Air
-Sun, Wind, Rain and Snow

Thunder and Lightning is a fictional story about the magical
land of Keenan, and the children who travel there.

Written, Printed and Bound in Canada

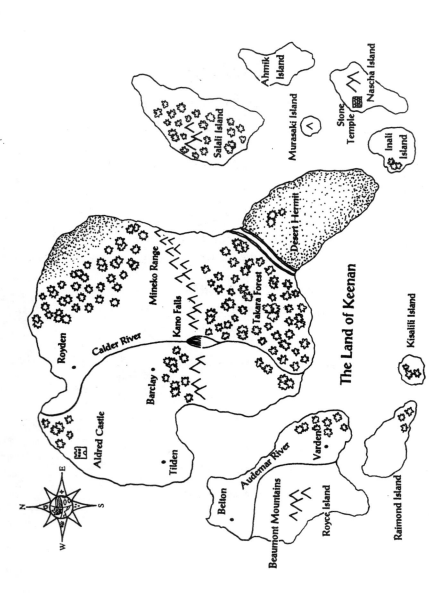

The Land of Keenan

Salali Island

Ahmik Island

Murasaki Island

Nascha Island

Stone Temple

Inali Island

Desert Hermit

Royden

Calder River

Mineko Range

Kano Falls

Takara Forest

Barclay

Aldred Castle

Tilden

Audemar River

Varden

Belton

Beaumont Mountains

Royce Island

Kisalili Island

Raimond Island

N · E · S · W

PART ONE

Excerpt from Elaine's Journal

January 26

Lately I have been wandering aimlessly around the local library. How can I explain to Mrs. Baird that the book I really want to sign out is actually in a castle library in another world.

I remember holding the huge leather volume titled The History of Keenan right in my hands. There wasn't enough time to read it then, but, oh, how I would love to read it now

It is the first time history has seemed so fascinating.

Chapter One

The Southern Shore
(on the edge of the
Takara Forest)
The Land of Keenan

The ancient Wizard slid very gingerly down the back of the giant sea creature. He stood knee deep in the water and patted the smooth gray hide of the beast gently.

"Thank you for helping me on my journey, Beriah," whispered the old man.

"I hope you find the one you are seeking," replied the creature.

"So do I, Beriah," said the Wizard. "I fear I shall soon be too old to climb on your back."

The creature's head was so enormous that he could only see the Wizard with the one eye that faced the land. The other eye looked out to sea. Beriah had seen many Wizards govern Keenan, most of them were annoying, but he liked this gentle man who always spoke so softly to him. Not everyone remembered how sensitive his hearing was out of water. He gazed at the Wizard, shocked to realize that he was indeed aging quickly. Time seemed so endless to the ageless sea creature.

"May I summon you again, Beriah," asked the Wizard politely.

The creature nodded solemnly and heaved its massive body back into the sea.

The Wizard stepped out of the water and stood dripping on the narrow sand at the edge of the forest. He flipped his long cape over his shoulders and searched the pockets in his dark blue tunic. When he found the right one, he extracted a small cloth bag. Opening the drawstring carefully, he removed a pinch of purple dust. He sprinkled the dust over his drenched leather boots. Instantly they were bone dry.

With a last glance at the sea, the Wizard entered the shadow of the forest. After a few paces, he selected a small twig from the forest floor. He removed another pinch of purple dust and rubbed it across the twig. Suddenly, the twig grew into a fine walking stick complete with a knobby handle at the top. It was a long stick, as the Wizard was an extremely tall man. He leaned on it heavily.

Reaching into another pocket, he pulled out a small brown leather book. The book had been passed down from Wizard to Wizard. Legends told how the First Wizard in Keenan had brought it from another world. The Wizard who had given it to him said it contained the magic of the First Wizard - a magic so powerful that it could still send help to Keenan. Although it was supposed to be a mysterious book, it had no intriguing title, and since he had owned the book, the pages had always been blank. So the Wizard was quite astonished when a few days ago, a map of the Takara Forest had magically appeared on the first page. It was roughly drawn in brown ink, and in the middle of the forest was a small thundercloud. It was very perplexing, and the Wizard had no idea what to make of it. All he could do was stare at the book, so that's all he did do for several days. Then yesterday as he studied the map, a poem had materialized right before his eyes.

Now standing in the dark forest, he leaned heavily on his stick, and holding the book carefully, he read it once again.

Hidden in the shadowlands,
Lives a self-crowned queen,
Ignoring Keenan's basic laws,
And filled with hate unseen.

She's lightning sharp,
          and lightning fierce,
And quick to strike a heart.
And you must use the opposite,
To bolt her realm apart.

The Wizard was deeply troubled that he didn't fully understand what he was supposed to do. He wondered why the book couldn't explain more to him. Then as he continued to think, he vaguely remembered a conversation he had had years ago between King Truman and one of his friends from another world.

The Wizard studied the hand-drawn map in the book closely. He wasn't sure how far into the forest he would find the Thundercloud, or if his idea was even right.

He hoped so, he definitely needed help, if it was up to him to fight the evil that threatened the land of Keenan.

Chapter two

Deep in the Takara Forest,
(on the mainland)
The Land of Keenan

Donar watched his mother grind the grains which she would use to make their bread. He pretended to be asleep so he could stay under his thick woolen blanket a bit longer. But his mother wasn't fooled.

"I need a fire son, and water from the stream. The sun is climbing and still my son thinks the moon is high."

"Yes, mother," said Donar as he rose and wrapped a dull gray coat around his shoulders. He picked up the water bucket and fingered the tree sap he had used to fill the hole. He wished they had something to trade for a new one. Then he took the coarse net bag that was hanging on its hook on the wall. It had taken him days to knot the twine to make it.

"Be kind to the part that carries you," said his mother. "Warm feet will travel further."

Donar nodded and wrapped two heavy woven mats around his bare feet and tied them into place. He kissed his mother's cheek and left their small mud hut.

On the way to the stream he gathered whatever twigs he could find, but he had traveled this path so often that loose wood was scarce. In his mind he convinced himself that he would have to leave his normal path to get more wood, but deep down he knew that what he really wanted to do was visit Orvin.

Orvin was the storyteller who lived in the village across the stream. When Donar was younger, his mother refused to let him visit the village, but as he got older she reluctantly allowed him to trade there. She never went to the village herself, and would not speak to him about it.

Most of the villagers were distantly polite to Donar, but Orvin was glad to have someone new to tell his stories to. Gradually Donar learned how very different his mother was from everyone at the village. Her way of speaking, which Donar had taken for granted as normal, was strange compared to everyone else. She walked differently too, almost regally. She even did her everyday chores very carefully and precisely. It was quite a contrast to the rough, loud, laughing village women, who didn't let a bit of dirt worry them.

Donar knew that he and his mother were much poorer than the villagers, which made the differences even more unusual. But learning about these things was nothing compared to the day that Orvin told him an absolutely astonishing story.

Many, many years ago, a stranger came to our small village. A beautiful woman in a long golden gown which flowed behind her like a river. Although she had rings on her fingers and elegant cloth, she had not food nor drink. Her weariness could not hide her beauty, and it was with this fairness that she captured the strongest of men in our village. He fed her and sheltered her and took her as his own. Although he may have thought he was richly favoured, a great tragedy soon befell him. The woman mourned his death, and finally her sadness took her away. It is a pity to say that not one was truly grieved to see her go. And even later, when the boy child was born, there was only his mother to greet him as he came into the world.

Orvin would not exactly come right out and say that the woman was Donar's mother, but Donar knew it was. It amazed Donar to think that his mother had actually lived in the village. He wished his mother would return to it, but he knew she would not, just as he knew she would never speak of why she left it.

His carrying bag was full of wood by the time Donar reached the bridge by the stream. As he reached the village clearing, he could tell at once that something was happening. A crowd had gathered and everyone was talking excitedly.

Donar was about to go closer when the crowd shifted and he saw a very grand man standing in the throng of people. He had a dark blue tunic and leggings and magnificent leather boots. He was quite tall and leaned heavily on a wooden walking stick. But the most impressive thing about this man was the flowing purple satin cape which was flung carelessly over his shoulders and fastened with a gold clasp.

Donar looked down at his makeshift shoes and dirty clothes, and he quickly backed up through the forest and silently made his way back home.

Chapter three

Donar didn't mention the man he had seen at the village to his mother, because then he would have to mention the fact that he went to the village. He didn't want to be the cause of his mother's frown.

As he made a fire and heated their breakfast, he watched his mother brush the dust off her most precious possession. It was a delicate tapestry woven from the finest silk threads. The scene depicted a field of purple flowers, and in the sky a storm was coming. The sky was so dark and the flowers so fresh and bright, that it made a startling contrast of colours. The silver lightning bolts shone vividly over the radiant blossoms, making the tapestry look extremely out of place against the mud wall of the shabby hut.

"Mother," called Donar. "Come and eat while the food is hot."

"I will, dear son. But first I must protect the beauty that protects my heart. For dust will damage the threads of the tapestry. Each thread has it own vital life which is important, but it also must hold the others in their place. When the threads obey the order of the tapestry just look at their amazing accomplishment."

"Yes mother," he sighed. "Now come and eat."

While they ate together, Donar's mind wandered. He wondered why such an important man would be at the small village so far from the Castle, for it must be from there that the man came. Orvin had told him stories about King Truman and the royal family at Aldred Castle in the high north. Orvin's stories had such vivid descriptions that Donar felt he could almost see the place. Once Donar asked him how he knew so much about far off places, when nobody in the village had ever left the Takara Forest, but Orvin refused to talk anymore that day. Donar never asked again, he didn't want to risk losing Orvin's friendship.

"Well my son, shall we pass our hours cultivating the soil that sustains us?"

"Yes Mother," replied Donar sighing again. He knew her gracious phrase really meant weeding the vegetable garden.

He watched his mother wrap a piece of dirty cloth around her clean dress. She carried another piece which she would spread on the dirt to kneel on. She tried so hard to stay neat and clean, and sometimes Donar wondered why, when nobody ever saw them.

"Do you require a cloth to protect your immaculate attire?" His mother grinned as she gazed at his filthy torn leggings.

Donar had to laugh, "No Madame, I believe I am suitably attired for my particular assignment." He gave a slight bow. His mother laughed out loud, and gave him a hug.

Around mid-day the forest was quiet, the animals were resting after a morning of foraging and Donar and his mother worked together silently. Suddenly Donar looked up. Although he couldn't see anything, he could hear the gentle crunch of footsteps. Someone was coming!

Donar looked at his mother for her reaction. He expected to see her disturbed frown or perhaps a surprised look, but what he saw made him tremble. His mother's eyes had filled with tears, which ran swiftly down her cheeks. She turned and gazed at him lovingly, then wiped her face on her skirt hem and ran her hands quickly

9

through her hair. Standing tall she waited to greet the first guest Donar could ever remember. And although it should have been quite the other way around, it was Donar who was surprised to see the grand man with the walking stick emerge from the trees. His mother showed no surprise at all.

Chapter four

"Hello Jurisa," said the man smiling at Donar's mother. "Is this your boy?"

"Of course," she replied. Donar was astonished at his mother's abruptness.

"What is his name?" inquired the man gently.

"Donar," she answered so quietly her words were almost lost among the rustling trees.

But the man heard, and his face lit up. "Donar. Donar. Oh yes, what a perfect name. Although if one wasn't aware of the meaning behind it, one would never guess. But perhaps that was your intention."

"I did as I was instructed," replied his mother quietly, but fiercely. "I named him."

"And now I did as I was instructed," said the man softly. "I found him."

"Yes," she said sadly. Then quite abruptly she turned and went inside the hut.

Donar who was absolutely astonished by this exchange, now studied the man intently. He couldn't ask all the questions swimming in his head all at once, so he settled for the obvious one.

"Who are you?"

The man smiled and extended his hand to Donar. "I am the Tenth Wizard of Keenan." He gripped Donar's hand warmly.

"How did you know my mother's name?" asked Donar.

"I met your mother long ago when she was just a girl at Aldred Castle," answered the Wizard.

"Oh, I think you are mistaken," said Donar. "My mother has never been to the castle."

The Wizard looked deeply at Donar, but he didn't reply. Suddenly Donar remembered the story Orvin told him. If the story really was about his mother, Orvin referred to her as a stranger who came to the village. Donar had never really thought past the part about her living in the village. Where had she come from? Could it be the Castle?

His mother returned with a tray of drinks and food. It seemed that even in her emotional state she didn't forget her manners. She placed the tray on a tree stump.

"Will you be departing soon?" she asked without looking into the Wizard's eyes.

"Yes, we will Jurisa," he replied tenderly. He placed his hand softly on hers.

She looked up at him. "He doesn't know. I'll need a few minutes alone."

"Of course," said the Tenth Wizard.

"Donar, come with me," demanded his mother.

He followed her into their hut. She sat him down on his sleeping platform. He looked at her nervously.

"Mother, what is happening?" asked Donar.

"You are an exceptional child. You have been chosen to help protect the Land of Keenan. Your fortune was decided long before your birth. You must now embark on the journey you were destined for," said his mother.

"I don't understand," he replied trembling.

"You must leave the forest and follow the Wizard. Assist him in all he asks, regardless how difficult or unreasonable it seems. This is your purpose in life."

"But Mother, I can't leave you. Who will gather your fire wood, and fetch your water? Who will help you in the garden?"

Donar was on the verge of tears. His emotions were tangling themselves up inside his stomach. An adventure with a Wizard - how exciting. Travelling away from home - how scary. Going off with someone he didn't know - how alarming. Leaving his mother alone - how worrisome.

"My son," said his mother, and at these tender words, her voice caught and she held him closely. "You must go, I have always known it. The Wizard is a good man. He will stay with you."

Donar lay his head on his mothers shoulder. When he saw the Wizard standing in the doorway, he let go, and stood up.

"Are you quite sure, Mother?" he asked.

"Yes, son," she replied.

"Very well Sir, I am ready," said Donar in what he hoped was a brave voice.

"I have nothing to send with him," said his mother sadly.

"Nothing is needed," said the Wizard kindly.

And somehow Donar managed to follow the Wizard through the familiar trees of the forest. He didn't look back, but he heard the quiet sob behind him, which seemed to echo in his heart.

Chapter five

Donar had a million questions in his head, but the further they walked away from anything that was familiar to him, the shyer he became. Watching the Wizard's satin cape billowing down his back, did nothing to improve his confidence.

"Have you ever been in this part of the forest Donar?" asked the Wizard.

"No Sir," replied Donar.

"Have you ever been to the sea?" asked the old man.

"No Sir," replied Donar.

"Oh dear," said the Wizard. "Donar you must not call me Sir all the time."

"I'm afraid I don't know your name Sir," explained Donar.

"Well, that's because I don't really have a name." The Wizard laughed at Donar's shocked face. "When I became a Wizard's apprentice, I had to give up my name. A Wizard has to give up all personal rights and work only for the good of Keenan. By giving up our names, we are reminded of this every day. Most of my friends call me Ten, because I am the Tenth Wizard. Will you call me Ten too?"

"Yes Sir," replied Donar.

As they traveled on, every so often, Ten would stop and lean on his walking stick, and take a little brown book out of one of his many pockets. While he studied his book, Donar took the time to re-adjust his lumpy, woven, tied-on shoes. He noticed one of the ties was wearing thin, and he wished he had thought to bring an extra one. Ten must have noticed it too, because he

14

looked down at Donar's feet and made a little clucking noise.

"Donar, you must let me provide you with some travelling clothes."

"Yes Sir Ten. I mean, if you think so," said Donar with his head down.

"Now that you are assisting me, it's the least I can do," said Ten.

Donar nodded, grateful for the Wizard's sensitivity.

"Now, where did I put it?" asked Ten to himself as he checked all his pockets.

Donar watched in amazement. Surely Ten didn't have some clothes in those tiny pockets. But finally the Wizard pulled out a small cloth bag and took a pinch of purple dust out. To Donar's surprise, he rubbed the dust into Donar's dirty leggings, then his old shirt, and finally his clumsy footwear. Suddenly Donar was wearing pale gray leggings, a dark gray tunic, and the same magnificent leather boots as the Wizard. He was so stunned he couldn't even reply.

"Hmm, not bad," said Ten with a smile. "But you'll be needing something to keep you warm at night." And with another pinch of dust, Donar had a handsome green cloak, made of heavy, sturdy cloth.

"Th-th-thank y-you Sir," stammered Donar. He was painfully aware how small those two words sounded. Never had he had such clothes. He felt quite unworthy of anything so grand, yet at the same time they made him feel so important.

Ten smiled happily at the boy's obvious pleasure. More and more he was feeling that this boy had to be part of the magic's plan.

15

It took awhile for Donar to get used to his new boots. It felt strange that he could no longer feel each twig and stone beneath his feet. He fairly pranced behind the Wizard, oblivious to his surroundings. But gradually he became aware of a new smell in the air. He was about to ask the Wizard what it meant, when he noticed the forest was coming to an end. Then suddenly before them was the shining sea.

"Isn't it beautiful?" asked Ten watching Donar's face. "We will make a fire and spend the night here."

Ten laughed at all the wood Donar collected from the forest's edge.

"All we need is one piece," he said, selecting a branch and placing it on the sand. He sprinkled the purple dust on it and - poof - a blazing fire appeared.

They settled down around it, warming their hands.

"Sir, ah, I mean Ten, how does that dust work?" asked Donar timidly.

"It's a magical powder made from the purple flowers of Murasaki Island. Wizards call it thinking dust. Whenever we think very hard about something the powder will make it happen. It is very handy and allows us to travel lightly."

"Oh," said Donar, but before he could ask anything else, Ten's dust poofed out two blankets. He handed one to Donar and curled up under the other one.

"Now, I am going to get an early rest. Tomorrow we will cross the sea and our quest will begin."

Chapter six

It was still light when Ten fell asleep, but too much had happened for Donar to lay down and stay still. Were they really going to cross the sea tomorrow? How would they get across?

He decided to climb one of the trees at the edge of the forest to get a better view of what lay beyond. The first branches were close together and easy to climb, but then they spread out and it was hard to get a grip. Stretching his hand out as far as he could go, he leaned one leg against the trunk of the tree. When he grasped the branch, he thrust the rest of his body away from the trunk. He made it to the higher branch, but he heard a sickening tearing sound. He had torn his brand new leggings! When he looked down and saw the size of the tear, he felt heartsick. Quickly scrambling down the tree, he made his way back to the fire. He sat there, with his heart pounding. What should he do? What could he do? What would the Wizard think, when he saw what he had done to his new clothes? Then he spied the small cloth bag. It had fallen out of the Wizard's pocket and was laying on the sand beside him. Maybe he could use the purple dust and concentrate on fixing his leggings. With a shaking hand he opening the drawstring and took a small pinch of dust. It felt dry and cold. He poised his hand over the tear, and closed his eyes. *Make the hole gone, make the hole gone,* he thought desperately. He sprinkled the dust. He felt cold air on his bare leg, and quickly opened his eyes. His leg was bare, for now the tear was gone, but a huge, neat hole replaced the jagged tear. Donar gazed at the hole in horror. Now what? Suddenly he felt the Wizard's eyes on him and he turned his head slowly.

Ten looked at his leggings and before Donar could get any words out, the Wizard asked a question.

"Did you use the magic dust?"

Donar nodded.

"Why?" asked Ten.

"I tore my leggings climbing a tree," whispered Donar.

"So you tried to fix them," said Ten. "What did you think when you sprinkled the dust?"

Donar's voice was shaky, but he managed to reply. "I thought - make the hole gone."

All at once Ten began to laugh. Donar looked up in amazement.

"Well," sputtered Ten, "the hole is gone. Do you see? The hole is gone."

Then suddenly Donar realized his mistake, he should have said, repair the hole or mend or fix.

"Donar," said Ten still laughing, "when you use magic, words are very important, and meanings are even more important. Now try again."

So taking another pinch of dust, Donar repaired the hole in his leggings perfectly. Ten smiled at him, but when the Wizard turned away to go back to sleep, his face looked serious. For he knew that the magical thinking dust only worked for Wizards.

Chapter seven

When Donar awoke, the Wizard had tea and crumpets with raspberry jam set out on a platter in front of the fire. Donar was delighted to join him for his first magical food. It was delicious.

"Where are we going Ten?" asked Donar between bites.

Ten studied Donar for a long time without replying. Finally he answered.

"I don't really know. In fact I'm not even sure what our quest really is."

"Oh," said Donar shocked.

"The thing is, Donar, all I know is what's in my book, and what is there isn't very clear."

"Oh," said Donar again.

"I suppose you think I'm not much of a Wizard," said Ten.

"Oh no," said Donar, "just the opposite. You're a great Wizard. I'm sure you'll figure everything out. And, well …"

"The opposite, you say," said Ten stroking his chin. "Ah, what were you saying?"

"I know I'm not very smart or anything, but since you were supposed to find me, maybe I can help you figure things out."

"I believe you're right," said Ten brightly.

He took a small brown leather book out of his pocket, and explained what it was to Donar. Then he showed him the map and the poem.

Donar read the poem:

Hidden in the shadowlands,
Lives a self-crowned queen,
Ignoring Keenan's basic laws,
And filled with hate unseen.

She's lightning sharp,
       and lightning fierce,
And quick to strike a heart.
And you must use the opposite,
To bolt her realm apart.

When he finished reading, he was stunned to see words writing by themselves on the blank page beside the first poem.

"Ten, I think you better look at this," he said.

Ten peered over his shoulder and they watched the brown ink write...

She wants to live forever,
But her aim is only strife.
Before destruction is complete,
She first must capture life.

She's lightning quick,
       and lightning mean,
So what to do - you wonder.
The only way to strike a strike,
Is with the sound of thunder.

"Do we have to fight this woman?" asked Donar.

"I believe that is the idea," answered Ten.

"She sounds mean," added Donar nervously. "Where is she?"

"That's the problem. I don't know."

"What is this Ten?" asked Donar pointing to the small thundercloud on the map of the first page of the book.

Ten looked at the map. The thundercloud wasn't in the Takara Forest anymore. It was right at the edge of the sea. Ten smiled. So my idea was right, he thought.

Donar interrupted his thoughts, "Ten. Look!"

Donar pointed to a tiny lightning bolt on the map. It was on Kisalili Island.

"Aha!" exclaimed Ten. "That must be where the evil lightning creature is. Now we know where to go. Good work, Donar."

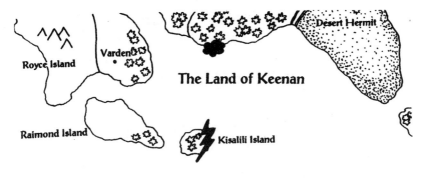

Donar smiled happily at the Wizards praise. Slowly his smile faded.

"Ten," he said. "If the person or creature we're searching for is represented by a lightning bolt on the map, and she is on Kisalili Island - then the thundercloud

21

must represent someone too. And if it does, then that someone must be nearby, because the symbol on the map is exactly where we are now!"

Ten looked at Donar in the strangest way, until Donar began to feel very uncomfortable. Ten opened his mouth to say something, and then closed it again. Donar thought perhaps he didn't want to know what Ten was trying to say. But then curiosity outweighed his fear.

"What is it?" Donar asked.

"Do you remember the conversation I had with your mother, when I asked her your name?" asked Ten.

"Yes, you said it was the perfect name," said Donar thinking back. "My mother also said she had done as she was instructed by naming me. What did she mean?" asked Donar remembering all the questions he had had.

"When your mother was a young girl at Aldred Castle, a visitor from another world told her that one day she would have a son. He said that the time would come when the boy would help Keenan through a great difficulty. He asked her to name her child Thunder, so he could be easily found when he was needed. The stranger made her promise with a sacred vow."

Donar, who had been getting a panicky feeling, now said with relief. "But my mother broke her promise, because my name is Donar, not Thunder."

"I think your mother was afraid, which was probably why she ran away from the castle. I'm sure she didn't really want you to be found. But she didn't break her promise. Donar is an old German name, which is a language from the stranger's world. It means - God of Thunder.

Donar, the thundercloud on the map is you."

PART TWO

Excerpt from Elaine's Journal

March 7

○

As my cousin, Zoe Amanda's birthday gets closer, I can't help thinking back to when she was born. When Zoe stopped breathing in the hospital, our family was devastated. None of us could bear to look ahead, in

○ case she didn't make it. But as soon as she was strong enough to come home, we all acted crazy with relief.

All the adults are still praising modern medicine continually. But I wonder what they would say if they knew the real reason Zoe is alive.

○

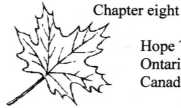

Chapter eight

Hope Town
Ontario
Canada

The phone rang. Elaine got up to answer it because her mother was doing a cross-stitch picture and she had embroidery floss spread all over her lap.

"Hello," said Elaine.

"Oh Elaine, thank goodness it's you," said an old whispery voice.

Elaine smiled when she realized it was Mrs. Nestor, but before she could reply, Mrs. Nestor hurried on.

"Is your Mom there? Don't let her know it's me. We have a problem Elaine. I need your help."

Elaine frowned.

"Who's on the phone, Elaine?" asked her mother.

"Just a friend for me," replied Elaine, hoping her mom would think it was someone from school. "I'm going to take this in my room."

"Ok," said her mother without looking up from her needlework.

"What's wrong?" asked Elaine as she closed the door to her room.

"Oh Elaine, your mother called me yesterday. She wants to bring your cousin Zoe over to my house for a visit next week."

"That sounds nice," said Elaine.

"No, it's not. It's terrible. She can't bring the baby here. It's far too dangerous," said Mrs. Nestor in a frightened voice.

"Dangerous!" exclaimed Elaine. "What on earth do you mean? How could your house be dangerous. Magical - yes, but not dangerous."

Even though Mrs. Nestor was the wisest adult Elaine knew, she thought Mrs. Nestor must be exaggerating. She was getting rather old.

"Elaine, are you listening? If baby Zoe comes here, we could lose her forever. There's so much about the magic that you still don't know. We can't take any chances. Elaine, what are we going to do?" asked Mrs. Nestor desperately.

"Don't worry," said Elaine. "I'll somehow change the plans. But I want to know what you are talking about. And this time don't tell me you don't have any answers because you are only the gatekeeper to the magical world of Keenan. I've felt all along that you know a lot more than you're letting on.

"Ok, I'll explain it, just don't let baby Zoe come anywhere near my house. You and your friends went through so much to save her, we can't lose her now. Promise me, you won't let it happen," pleaded the old lady.

"I promise," said Elaine.

"Thank you. We'll talk more about this later," said Mrs. Nestor.

Oh yes, thought Elaine as she hung up the phone, we'll definitely talk more. And then she raised one eyebrow, the way she always did, when she was on the verge of a magical discovery.

Chapter nine

Elaine sat on the front porch, huddled in her coat. She was waiting for Adam to come over. Even though there was still snow on the ground, she could feel the spring air starting to stir. She looked down the road, wondering if Adam would walk over or ride his bicycle. The ice on the gravel road that led to Adam's farm had finally melted, so maybe he would ride his bike. She was lucky that her best friends lived so close. Brooke lived four houses down from Elaine, and Clark had just moved to Hope Town last year. The four friends were very close. It was a closeness that was made stronger by the magical adventures they had shared.

While she was waiting, Elaine allowed her mind to wander back to the time she and her friends had discovered that old Mrs. Nestor's grandfather clock was actually a passageway to the land of Keenan --- a world outside the time and space of the world they lived in. In their first visit, the four friends had helped a Wizard save the dying magic of Keenan. Elaine's heart still pounded with excitement every time she thought of it.

Her thoughts were interrupted when she saw Adam walking down the road. She ran over to meet him and started explaining her strange conversation with Mrs. Nestor as they walked back to Elaine's house.

"Did Mrs. Nestor explain why Zoe couldn't visit?" asked Adam.

"No, but she said she would explain why it was so dangerous. She admitted that there's a lot she hasn't told us," said Elaine.

"Do you think she really will?" asked Adam as he sat down at Elaine's kitchen table. "You know how mysterious Mrs. Nestor is. I doubt we'll ever learn all there is to know about her or her magical old Elvina House."

"Yes, she'll have to tell us something," said Elaine. "You didn't hear how upset she was about Zoe coming to visit. It must be something really important. I wish I knew what it was right now."

"Do you think it has anything to do with when we went to Keenan to ask for the medicine?" asked Adam.

"I don't know," said Elaine.

They both thought back to their second visit to Keenan. Right after Zoe was born, she stopped breathing. The doctors hooked the baby up to all kinds of machines to keep her breathing, but they didn't think Zoe would live. Elaine knew their only chance was the magic of Keenan. It wasn't easy to get back, and when they finally did get there, they found all sorts of trouble in the land. They ended up having to search the Eastern Islands to replenish the Wizard's magical ingredients, before he could make the medicine.

Adam looked at Elaine. She was staring at a photo of Zoe on the refrigerator. He smiled at her.

"Zoe's birthday's coming up soon, isn't it?" he asked.

"Yes," she said smiling. Then she frowned. "What do you think could be so dangerous?"

"I don't know Elaine, said Adam with a worried look. "How are you going to stop Zoe from visiting Mrs. Nestor's house? And, what are you going to tell your mother?"

"What are you going to tell your mother about what?" asked Elaine's mother as she appeared suddenly in the kitchen doorway.

Elaine couldn't help smiling at Adam's surprised and then apologetic face. But Elaine had already thought of an idea, so she thought she would have some fun.

"I guess I'll have to tell her the truth," she said very seriously.

Elaine hoped her mother wouldn't notice Adam's shocked disbelief. None of their parents knew anything about the adventures they had had in another world. In fact, the only adult who knew anything about Keenan was Mrs. Nestor.

"Well Mom, I was talking with Mrs. Nestor and she doesn't want us to visit her next week."

"Whatever do you mean?" asked Mrs. Maddock. "She seemed so pleased when I called."

"Actually she wants to see us, but she had a pipe burst in her kitchen and her whole place is a mess," explained Elaine, grinning at Adam's relieved face. "I guess she's kind of embarrassed about it. You know how fussy she is about her decor."

"My goodness," replied Mrs. Maddock. "Why didn't she just ask if she could come here instead."

"Mom," exclaimed Elaine faking a disapproving look, "inviting yourself to someone's home - that isn't proper."

Mrs. Maddock smiled. "She is rather old fashioned, isn't she? It's so rare to find someone with such old world charm."

"You mean Old Worlds charm," said Elaine with a grin. But her mother wasn't paying attention.

"I'd better call her right now and extend an invitation here," said Mrs. Maddock.

Now it was Elaine's turn to be surprised. She hadn't had time to warn Mrs. Nestor about the excuse she had made up. She glanced desperately at Adam and luckily he understood.

"Why Mrs. Maddock," he exclaimed peering at the jumble of threads and patterns that covered the kitchen table, "are you working on a new cross-stitch picture?"

Mrs. Maddock beamed at him as she started showing him samples from a book. Elaine excused herself and ran to the phone in her mother's bedroom. She pressed Mrs. Nestor's number from memory.

"Hi, it's Elaine. My mom's going to call you and invite you here because of all the water damage at your place from the burst pipe," said Elaine in a rush.

"Elaine," replied Mrs. Nestor in a stern voice, "you lied to your mother!"

"It was all I could think of. What did you want me to say?"

"You're right," said Mrs. Nestor, "under the circumstances it can't be helped. We must go to any lengths to save Zoe's life ... again."

Chapter ten

The next day, Elaine lugged a big picnic basket out to the treehouse in the forest behind her house. She hung on to the rope handrail with one hand and carried the basket up the ramp with the other. It was a cloudy day and inside the treehouse, the green plastic roof made it darker. She heard footsteps and peered out the window. She saw Brooke hurrying along through the trees.

"I can't believe we're meeting outside today. It's so cold," moaned Brooke puffing as she climbed the ramp.

"I can't believe you're the first one here. Did you see Adam and Clark on the way over?" asked Elaine.

"No," said Brooke wrapping her scarf tighter around her neck.

"Do you want something to eat?" asked Elaine.

"Wow, you brought food. Great," exclaimed Adam standing in the treehouse doorway.

"I don't know how you always manage to sneak up on us," said Brooke.

Adam dug into the picnic basket and was eating a sandwich when Clark rushed in.

"What did I miss?" asked Clark. Then he spied the basket. "Did you leave any food for me? What's in there?"

Elaine sighed. "We're here to make plans, not eat."

"Oh yes, you said something about it being dangerous for Zoe to go to Mrs. Nestor's house. What's that all about?" inquired Clark.

"Dangerous!" shouted Brooke. "Now what's going on?"

"Pass the sandwiches," said Clark with a mouthful of cookies.

"I'm not doing anything dangerous," announced Brooke firmly.

"Elaine, do you have a pen?" asked Adam. "I want to make some notes about what we know about the Elvina House so far."

Elaine passed Adam a pen, and peered over his shoulder at his journal notes. Adam had always recorded anything to do with their adventures, and Elaine had to admit his notes had helped them a lot.

"So tell us the news," pleaded Clark.

"Are we going to try to go to Keenan again?" asked Brooke nervously.

"The first thing we have to do, is get to Mrs. Nestor's house," answered Elaine.

"Oh, is that all? Well, that's all right," agreed Brooke.

"But after that, who's knows," said Elaine grinning at Brooke.

Chapter eleven

Elaine's nerves were frazzled. After they had finally bribed one of Adam's brothers to drive them over to Mrs. Nestor's house, they had to go through the painfully slow process of making tea, before they could talk.

Mrs. Nestor's tiny parlour always seemed too small when the four of them visited. Adam sat on a tiny stool with wooden legs carved to resemble lion's paws. Elaine paced back and forth which was difficult as she could only take three steps each way.

"Sit down Elaine," said Adam. "You're making me crazy, and you're going to break something." He looked around nervously at all the china knick-knacks on the fragile little tables.

Brooke entered carrying a china platter edged with gold, and filled with cookies. Clark followed her closely. Then finally Mrs. Nestor appeared with a tray full of fancy tea cups. She poured the tea, and sat back gazing at the four children with a serious look. Everyone was quiet while Mrs. Nestor stirred her tea carefully. Just when Adam thought Elaine was going to burst, Mrs. Nestor started to talk.

"We have some serious things to discuss today, so we'd better get to it. I'm sure you are wondering why I'm going to tell you things today, that I didn't tell you before. As you well know, I am the gatekeeper of the passage from our world to the Land of Keenan, and as a gatekeeper I took a vow of secrecy. The only reason I am breaking my vow is because I fear for baby Zoe. When Elaine found the Brown Leather Book in my late husband's study, she didn't know anything about me or this house. The reason I gave her the Wizard's book was because I knew she had found it for a reason. The book would not have let itself be found by anyone who wasn't supposed to see it. It's far too magical for that. What I didn't know until the four of you had figured it out, was that each of you represent one of the four elements of the ancient universe."

As she spoke, Adam, who had his journal with him, turned to the page where he had recorded the discovery of the meaning of their names, and their horoscopes.

FIRE
: Elaine means light (Greek)
Maddock means fire (Celtic)
Elaine is a Leo (Fire Element)

WATER
: Brooke means stream (Old English)
Coburn means small stream (Old English)
Brooke is a Pisces (Water Element)

EARTH
: Adam means red earth (Hebrew)
Boliston means earth (Greek)
Adam is a Taurus (Earth Element)

AIR
: Clarence (Clark's real name) means clear (Latin)
Zoltan means life (Greek)
Clark is a Libra (Air Element)

"I'm not sure if you realize," continued Mrs. Nestor, "but the first Wizard of Keenan set up restrictions to keep people from other worlds from entering Keenan."

"We did know that, Mrs. Nestor," interrupted Elaine. "The Eighteenth Wizard told us when we were in Keenan."

"But he didn't tell us how or why," said Adam.

"I don't know how," replied Mrs. Nestor, "but I know one reason was to keep out newcomers who could badly influence or harm Keenan's inhabitants."

"Wait a minute," said Elaine. "I know that we weren't the only human elements to visit Keenan. But just because we're elements doesn't mean we're not going to hurt Keenan in some way."

"But," replied Mrs. Nestor, "as elements, you were specially chosen. Also, anytime you have a group, each member of the group has some control over the group itself. The elements always total four, and they must enter Keenan together. If one of you had thoughts of harming Keenan while you were there, the other three would have probably stopped you."

"Oh," said Adam, with understanding. "That's clever."

"I have a question," said Elaine.

"What dear?" asked Mrs. Nestor.

"Your husband wasn't an element, and he wasn't part of a group, so how did he get into Keenan?"

"My Elwin, bless his soul, had a friend who gave him some seeds to plant in the garden. They were beautiful purple flowers that bloomed and spread and eventually surrounded our house."

"The lilacs," breathed the children together. For it was those magical flowers that helped transport them to Keenan.

"Yes, the lilacs," said Mrs. Nestor. "The flowers from Keenan. My husband was always a great believer, magical ideas flowed through him all his life. Being close to the lilacs gave him the power to travel to Keenan. Some people are just that way, always open to the power of suggestion and able to make their dreams a reality. Some people can walk through a magical gateway whenever they try, and sometimes without trying at all."

"Oh," whispered Elaine suddenly.

"Sometimes my husband went to the kitchen to make a pot of tea and disappeared for hours, even days."

"Wait," said Adam interrupting. "The first time we went to Keenan, we traveled through the door of the grandfather clock. But when we tried to go back to ask the Wizard for medicine to save Zoe, the clock's door wouldn't work."

"That's right," said Clark. "We had to go through the attic stairway, and your husband went through the kitchen door. Does that mean my idea was right - that you can't use the same passage twice?"

"No Clark," said Mrs. Nestor. "What I'm trying to tell you, is that the whole house is a passageway. Every entrance door, closet door, cabinet door, even the gate in the back garden is an entrance to Keenan."

"Then why was it so hard for us to get there?" asked Brooke.

"Because you are elements," explained Mrs. Nestor, "and you need to go through the same door, at the same time, while being physically connected to each other and have a magical connection. But for a magical person like my husband, all he had to do was walk through a door alone, and at any time he could be transported. He, himself, was a magical connection."

"Mrs. Nestor, are you going to explain what makes a person magical enough for this to happen to?"

asked Elaine quietly, even though she thought she knew the answer.

Mrs. Nestor smiled, because she knew Elaine had already guessed. "I believe that someone who's life was saved by the Wizard's magical medicine, and someone who was baptized by the waters from Keenan's river could quite possibly qualify."

"That's baby Zoe!" exclaimed Brooke.

"Yes Brooke," said Mrs. Nestor patiently. "That's baby Zoe."

Chapter twelve

Even though Elaine knew that Mrs. Nestor was going to tell them that Zoe was at risk, she still shivered when she heard her cousin's name. She was also fascinated with the fact that every doorway in Mrs. Nestor's house was a passageway to Keenan.

"Wait a minute," said Clark. "Zoe can't even walk yet. How could she go through a passageway by herself?"

Mrs. Nestor frowned. "She can still crawl, but even if she couldn't, imagine Elaine's Aunt Meredith carrying Zoe in her arms, but when she enters the parlour, suddenly Zoe's not there."

Everyone silently considered the terrible possibility. When Elaine pictured Zoe lost and alone in an unfamiliar place filled with danger, she shuddered violently.

"So now you see why we must keep Zoe away from this house," said Mrs. Nestor stirring her second cup of tea.

The five of them agreed to do everything possible to prevent that from happening. Elaine felt confident that they could keep Zoe safe. She also felt excited. Her mind kept going over the fact that every door was a way to her beloved magical land.

"Mrs. Nestor," asked Elaine, "does this mean if we held hands, and walked into the kitchen at the same time, holding your magical lilacs, we could get to Keenan right now?"

"I don't know," replied Mrs. Nestor. "I suppose it's possible if you had a strong enough magical connection."

"Oh," said Elaine with a hopeful sigh.

37

"Too bad we don't have the magical Brown Leather Book with all the poems in it," said Clark.

"We still have the poems, even if we don't have the book," said Adam holding out his journal.

Elaine held the journal, remembering the magical time when they had stood in front of the grandfather clock and recited the poem. She read the lines again.

It seems that there are only four,
Windows through the land,
Windows that become a door,
For those who understand...

"Mrs. Nestor, I'm confused about something," said Elaine. "The poem says there are only four doors to Keenan. I had figured the clock was one and the stairway to the attic was another. In fact I had come to the conclusion that if Clark was right and we couldn't travel through the same door twice, maybe we only had two more chances to visit Keenan. But if every doorway is a passage, your house has more than four doors. So what does the poem mean?"

"My goodness, Elaine. You sure don't make it easy to keep my vow of secrecy." Mrs. Nestor stared at them for a few moments. Then she sighed and continued. "Actually this whole house is considered to be one door. There are three others located somewhere else in our world."

"Really," said Brooke. "Do you know where they are?"

"I only know of one other," said Mrs. Nestor.

"Where is it?" asked Clark.

"In the small town of Dudleigh, England," replied Mrs. Nestor.

"That figures," said Adam. "Of course it would be England."

"Why?" asked Brooke.

"When we were first researching information about other worlds, every book we read was written in England. Remember Elaine?" said Adam.

"Yes," she answered. "We figured Ontario was the most unmagical place that ever existed. Wow, were we wrong. Well is everybody ready?" she asked jumping up from her delicate chair, making it wobble precariously.

"Ready for what?" asked Brooke

"To try and get to Keenan, of course."

Chapter thirteen

"You want to go to Keenan right this very minute?" asked Brooke nervously.

"Of course," said Elaine. "Is it all right, Mrs. Nestor?"

"If you like dear," smiled Mrs. Nestor.

"Can I pack a couple of turkey sandwiches first?" asked Clark. "Maybe some ham and salami too."

"I'm not sure I'm ready to go," said Brooke. "For one thing I'm wearing a dress. Maybe I should go home and change."

"Oh please, how the three of you became elements is beyond me," growled Elaine.

"Hey, I'm ready," said Adam offended.

"Thank goodness," said Elaine smiling at him.

Elaine's smile always made him feel hot. "Come on," he said to the others. "Let's try."

Elaine tucked the lilac-filled sachet that Mrs. Nestor handed her, into the pocket of her jeans so she had her hands free. The four friends held hands together and repeated the magical poem. They squashed together so they could walk into the kitchen at the same time. But when they passed through the doorway they only saw Mrs. Nestor's old fashion wood stove, and the gingham cloth on her little round table.

"The magic just isn't strong enough," said Elaine sadly. "Remember how terribly strong the smell of the lilacs were before? These sachets have lost their strength," she complained sniffing them loudly.

"Maybe we need fresh lilacs," said Adam.

"I don't think that's the problem," said Clark.

"What do you mean?" asked Adam.

40

"Each time we got into Keenan, there was a problem in the land, that we helped solve. I think the reason we made it to Keenan was that Keenan called us, not that we tried to get there," explained Clark.

Adam was amazed at Clark's words. He felt strongly that Clark was probably right. He looked at Elaine to see what she was thinking. Deep in her heart Elaine suspected that Clark was right, but she didn't want to admit it. Adam knew how hard it would be for Elaine to agree.

"Elaine, it's probably just as well that we don't get there right now. It would be terrible if we didn't get home in time and your mom brought Zoe over here looking for us," said Adam, giving Elaine a reason to stop trying.

Brooke, who could sense Elaine was on the verge of tears, swallowed hard and said, "Come on everyone, let's try again."

That day Elaine, Brooke, Adam and Clark walked through every door in Mrs. Nestor's house. Elaine even tried to climb into a small curio cupboard, but nothing ever happened.

PART THREE

Excerpt from Elaine's Journal

March 10

We spent the day at Mrs. Nestor's house trying to get back to Keenan, with no luck at all.

I often think of my friends there, especially Eighteen. Part of my reason for wanting to go back is to see them again, even though I know deep in my heart, they probably won't be there. If only their time didn't flow so much faster than ours...

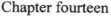

Chapter fourteen

The Southern Shore
(on the edge of the
Takara Forest)
The Land of Keenan

"How will we get to Kisalili Island, Ten?" asked Donar gazing out at the brilliant water.

"Wait and see," replied Ten mysteriously as he searched his many pockets.

Donar was intrigued when Ten dropped purple petals into the sea. He watched them swirl around until they floated out of sight. Soon a large dark shape appeared just below the water's surface.

"That's Beriah," said Ten. "He's going to carry us to the island. But you must always remember to speak extremely quietly to him. His hearing is very sensitive."

"Wow!" exclaimed Donar in a quiet whisper. "He's huge." Donar didn't think he would forget to be quiet. This was a creature he didn't want to make angry.

The giant sea creature heaved himself on the sand and greeted the Wizard gruffly. After Ten explained where they needed to go, Donar asked in a hushed whisper if he could pat his back.

"I suppose," said Beriah grumpily. "You might as well just climb up. Will that be close enough for you to harass me then?"

The Wizard was very pleased that the sea creature didn't mind an extra passenger.

"At least the small human spoke softly, that's something anyway," said Beriah.

"Thank you, Beriah," said Ten.

43

"The smaller they are, the louder they are... usually..." Beriah mumbled to himself as they lurched into the sea.

Donar was delighted to be sailing over the water in such a wonderful way. The water that sloshed up their legs was cold, but the sun was warm and the ride was gentle.

They passed two other shores, both filled with trees. Donar stretched to get a better look but he couldn't see much.

About a hundred feet away from their destination, Beriah stopped. Donar could see the huge jagged rocks near the shore that prevented Beriah from getting any closer.

"Get lost now humans. I'm certainly not going to shred myself to bits just to get you to shore," Beriah grumbled.

"Jump in, Donar," said Ten quietly. "We'll wade in from here." Ten had a feeling Beriah was acting so grumpy to impress Donar. He tried not to smile as they both climbed down and went around to Beriah's face to thank him.

"Will I see you again?" asked Donar in a hushed awed voice.

"No doubt you'll need me to drag you somewhere else sometime," replied the creature and without even a nod good-bye, he dove back to deeper water and sank down out of sight.

The water only reached Ten's waist, but it was up to Donar's chest, and it was freezing. If it had seemed cold splashing their feet, that was nothing compared to standing in it.

"Come on," said Ten shivering. "Let's hurry."

44

It was hard work trying to get around the rocks and soon their bodies felt numb.

"Don't worry," said the Wizard encouragingly. "When we reach the shore we'll think ourselves warm and dry."

"Does the powder still work when it's wet?" asked Donar with his teeth chattering.

"Yes," said Ten huffing.

All at once, Donar had the strangest feeling that they weren't alone, but before he could even turn his head, he felt his whole body being lifted out of the water. A huge green scaly thing with yellow stripes had tightened around his chest, making it so hard to breath he could hardly yell.

Chapter fifteen

"Help!" screamed Donar, as he pounded on the green scales violently. He felt the pressure loosen and he looked around for Ten. Surely a Wizard could save him. But what he saw made his heart tremble. For there was Ten, gripped tightly by two enormously sharp claws. He too, was out of the water, his legs dangling uselessly, and his arms waving in desperation.

Donar looked up and finally saw the monster's head high above them. He realized it was the monster's tail that held him so tightly.

"Donar, are you all right?" gasped Ten.

"What is this thing?" called Donar in fright.

"It's a sea dragon. I thought they were extinct. What are we going to do?" moaned Ten.

Oh great, he's asking me, thought Donar in despair. Then a shadow fell over them and Donar saw the dragon's deep red wings spread above them.

"Silence!" roared the sea dragon. "Who dares to disturb my abode?"

"Please," pleaded Ten. "We didn't mean to bother..."

But his words were drowned by an evil roar that shook Donar to his very core.

"I do not tolerate strangers in my territory. You have tempted fate, and you have lost. Now you will die."

Donar looked at Ten in despair. He saw blood dripping from Ten's chest where the dragon's claws were cutting his skin. Ten wouldn't meet his eyes. At that moment Donar knew it was up to him to save them. But what could he do? The sea dragon's tail was tightening again. He could hardly breathe. He thought of his

46

mother. *Think*, she told him. *There's always an answer.* He started to feel lightheaded. His lungs gasped frantically for air. It was too late to think. But then, out of nowhere, an idea came.

"Ten," croaked Donar, "throw me the thinking dust."

Ten's head drooped over his chest, which was covered in blood now.

"Ten!" screeched Donar. "Throw me the dust. Please!"

Finally Ten moved, as if in slow motion. His hand lifted to his shredded, bloody, pocket and he grabbed the small cloth bag. With his last bit of strength, he flung the bag toward Donar. Donar's trembling hand caught the edge of the bag. He ripped it open and dumped the dust over the green and yellow scaly tail. He rubbed it in and thought as hard as he ever had in his life.

Make this creature nice, kind, gentle, friendly, good and caring.

Then everything went black.

Chapter sixteen

Every breath he took hurt, but the tightness was finally lifted off his chest. He realized he was lying on something cold and wet. Donar opened his eyes. He saw the terrifying face of the sea dragon staring down at him. He shuddered, then winced as a pain shot through him with every breath he took. At any moment he would feel the claws that attacked Ten. He closed his eyes. He waited. Nothing happened. He opened his eyes again.

"Are you all right?" asked a kind voice with dreadfully smoky breath.

Donar opened his eyes wider. Was that who he thought it was? The sea dragon's face came into closer view.

"Dear young human, can you speak?"

"Yes," said Donar uncertain what was going on. Then he remembered the thinking dust. It must have worked!

"I am so sorry," said the dragon remorsefully. "I don't know what came over me. I hope you can forgive me." A tear shone in his yellow eyes, and then evaporated into stream.

"It's ok," said Donar in relief.

"Really?" asked the dragon cheerfully. "Oh I am glad. I hope we can be friends. My name is Alkuluki."

"Hello. How do you do," said Donar absurdly. Suddenly he remembered how badly hurt Ten was. "Where is my friend?" he asked fearfully.

"Over there," said Alkuluki, pointing with a razor sharp claw.

Donar shuddered as he followed the claw. He saw Ten lying on the sand a few yards away. Shivering with cold, Donar ran over to the Wizard. He felt sick when he saw the amount of blood on Ten's chest.

"Ten," he called, shaking the Wizard's shoulders. "Ten. Oh, please answer me."

Finally Ten opened his eyes. He started shaking.

"Donar, get the thinking dust. Make us dry."

Donar gulped. "I can't," he said quietly.

"Why not?" croaked Ten.

"I used it up on the sea dragon," explained Donar.

"What?" asked Ten confused.

"That's why he let us go," said Donar.

Ten looked up at the huge creature in surprise. "He's still here. Why hasn't he killed us?"

Donar leaned over and whispered in Ten's ear, "Because I *thought* him nice."

Ten looked at Donar in amazement. "That's brilliant!"

"I guess so," said Donar, staring at the small empty bag in dismay.

Chapter seventeen

One thing Donar knew how to do quite well without magic was make a fire. He gathered the wood and rubbed two sticks together until a tiny stream of smoke appeared. Then he blew gently until the smoke had caught the dead leaves on one of the branches he had gathered. Soon he had a blazing fire.

Then he gently removed Ten's tunic and spread it beside the fire to dry. Ten's chest was covered in holes, and most were still bleeding. He needed something to wash the blood away and bind Ten's chest. He removed his wonderful cape and looked at it regretfully for a moment before he tried to rip it up. But the coarse fabric that had kept him so warm was too thick to rip.

"Hey Alkuluki," he called. "Could you use your claws to rip my cape into strips for bandages?"

"Certainly friend. I'm very glad to be of help," replied the sea dragon happily.

Donar laid his cape on the sand and held it as the terrible claws sliced the cloth into neat rows. Then Donar cleaned Ten's wounds with sea water and tied the strips of cloth tightly around his chest. Soon the fire had dried them both and Ten was even sitting up.

Ten looked through the pockets of his torn tunic in despair. Most of them were completely shredded. There was nothing left.

Donar felt sick. "I'm really sorry Sir. I 've lost all the magic."

"Oh Donar," replied Ten. "I'm the one who should be sorry. I risked your life and you..." he faltered, but then continued. "You saved mine. You used your head in a crisis. You made a fire. You tended to my wounds. I have relied on magic for so long, that I've forgotten how to do things for myself. What are we going to do now?"

"I think we should find a place for you to rest and gain your strength," said Donar looking at the trees. "We don't know who we might find on this island or who might find us."

"Excuse me," interrupted the sea dragon. "I know of a hut that a human lived in long ago. Perhaps you could rest there."

"Are you sure nobody lives there now?" asked Donar.

"Oh yes, it's quite deserted," Alkuluki replied.

Donar suddenly wondered where the person was, and how the dragon knew he wasn't there. He decided not to ask any more questions.

"It's quite close," said the sea dragon leaning his head closer to them.

Donar held his breath against the horrible smell of the smoky creature.

"You had better lean back," he said cautiously. "You might burn us."

"Oh dear, yes. That would be dreadful. Well, the hut is just beyond the grove of birch trees behind you. I should go now. Please accept my apology for so rudely harming you. If there's anything I can ever do to help you, I am at your service. Good-bye small humans."

Then Alkuluki folded up his red wings and ducked his head into the water. His long scaly tail shot up into the air and then slid down beneath the water, and he was gone.

For a long time Donar and Ten just sat beside the fire without talking. Donar's bones felt sore and he didn't want to move. He knew Ten must be hurting even more.

Finally Donar gave a long branch of fire to Ten to hold while he put out the remaining fire with the surrounding sand. Then he grasped the torch with one hand and took Ten's arm with the other. Slowly they headed to the birch trees.

They found the hut easily. It was almost identical to Donar's home and his heart lurched when he saw it. They called and knocked but it seemed deserted as Alkuluki promised, so they went in.

Inside they found a table and two benches, a sleeping platform with several dusty blankets, and a fire pit. There was also a large curtain hanging on the back wall. Donar put the fire in the pit, shook the blankets outside, and then helped Ten get comfortable on the platform. Donar knew that it was up to him to keep things going now. There would be no more magical food and magical fires, but he wasn't worried. He knew exactly what to do now - the same things he had done every day of his life. He watched Ten turn over and start to snore. Then Donar went out to gather fire wood. He boiled sea water in the large pot he found by the fire pit. He picked some nearby fruit and placed it on the table for later. When all his chores were done, he joined Ten and fell fast asleep.

Chapter eighteen

Ten was surprised and delighted to wake up to a warm fire, a cup of water and fresh fruit. They sat at the mysterious person's table and talked about what they should do next.

"Why don't you check your Wizard's book? Maybe there's something new in it that will help us," suggested Donar.

"I can't," replied Ten sadly.

"Oh no!" exclaimed Donar. "Was it in your tunic too?"

"It was. Now it's somewhere in the sea." Ten put his head down on the table.

He didn't look like the grand Wizard that he was when Donar first saw him. His beautiful purple satin cape was dirty and ragged and looked ridiculous over his bandages. His boots were scuffed and his leggings were dirty. In fact, he looked a lot like Donar usually looked, except that Donar had cleaned himself up this morning. He had washed his new clothes carefully last night and even though he didn't have his cape, he looked quite presentable.

"I'm sorry about your book. I know how important it was to you. But we can't give up now. I think we should sneak around the island and try and find out who lives here."

"I suppose," agreed Ten reluctantly.

They walked through the trees as quietly as they could until they found a small clearing surrounded by berry bushes. If this place was anything like home, Donar knew that eventually people would come by. He also didn't think Ten was up to walking very far, so they decided to hide behind the bushes and wait to see if anything would happen.

It was a long time before their patience paid off. They heard the quiet rumble of voices before they could see anybody. Then they heard the rustle of branches as two people came into sight. Donar was so astonished at the sight of them, it took him a while to figure out that they were children. They were in fact, a brother and sister going about the ordinary task of picking berries. The reason Donar was so surprised had to do with the colour of their skin and hair. The children were green. Their skin was the bright leaf green of a tender new plant. Their hair was the dark green of a shady forest. They were very short and stocky. Donar and Ten watched the children for awhile. The boy seemed to eat more berries than he collected and the girl scolded him. Soon they drifted away.

It wasn't long before the bushes rustled again and another green person came by. She was quite a bit older, but not much taller than the others. She crept over to the bushes nervously, looking over her shoulder constantly in all directions, as if to make sure she was alone. Donar felt her apprehension and it made him feel uneasy too.

Suddenly there was a whisper coming from the bushes on the other side of the girl. She cleared her throat twice, and then someone emerged carefully from the bushes. It was a boy. An orange boy. His skin and hair were the colour of a ripe pumpkin. He was short too, and squat with wide shoulders. He looked around carefully and then rushed towards the girl. Tenderly, he took her hands in his own. She turned her face up to his, and gazed lovingly into his eyes. They whispered quietly to each other.

Donar turned away from them. He felt this was a private conversation and he didn't want to intrude. Ten smiled at his sensitivity and turned away as well.

After the young people left, there was nobody else for a long time. Donar and Ten drank from the flask they had found in the hut and ate berries from the bushes. Just when they were ready to give up, they heard a small branch snap.

Much to their surprise, a tiny face peeked through the low branches of the bushes. It was a vivid purple face belonging to a baby. By now Donar wasn't the least bit surprised to see such a colour of skin. The baby only had the tiniest tuft of hair but of course it was purple too. The little face smiled and gurgled at them, not showing any fear of strangers.

"Who are you talking to now, my little sweetie?" an unseen voice asked the baby. "Have you seen another squirrel?"

Then the green face of a woman peered over the bushes. She gasped loudly, and grabbed the baby with the swift movement of a terrified mother.

"Please Madame, don't be afraid. We won't harm you," pleaded Ten.

By the time he had stood up, the child had been completely wrapped in a blanket and covered from head to toe. If Donar and Ten hadn't seen the baby, they wouldn't have guessed there was a baby in the woman's trembling arms.

"We won't hurt you or your little baby," said Ten again.

"Please don't tell anyone," begged the woman. "Oh dear," she stammered. Then she fell to the ground and began to cry.

Ten looked so appalled that Donar went over to the woman and sat down beside her.

"Why are you crying?" he asked.

"Because you've come to take her away," she sobbed.

Donar looked at Ten in astonishment.

"She thinks we want her baby," said Ten in surprise.

"We don't want your baby," said Donar to the woman. "We're strangers here, but we mean no harm."

The woman looked up. "You don't work for Asnee then?" she asked.

"No," said Donar.

"I thought you were her spies. We're all afraid of her." The baby wiggled in the blanket and the woman allowed the tiny purple face to peek out.

"Who is Asnee?" asked Ten.

"She's the ruler of Kisalili Island. She calls herself the Lady of Lightning."

Chapter nineteen

"Where does Asnee live?" asked Donar.

"Up on the hill near Hailstorm Rock," replied the green woman.

"Can you take us there?" asked Donar.

"Oh no," she replied hastily. "I don't want to get flashed. You should stay away too."

"What do you mean - get flashed?" asked Ten.

"That's what she does to people who don't follow her rules. She points at them with her finger and a silver light flashes at them, and then they're gone forever. Only a little pile of dust is left on the ground where they were."

"Oh," said Donar in horror.

"Anyway," said the woman, "I have to be getting home before the storm tonight."

"Oh, it won't storm tonight," said Donar. "Look how clear the sky is. There isn't a cloud in sight."

"Well, now I know you really are strangers here. Perhaps you should come home with me. You can shelter in my hut until the storm is over," said the woman kindly.

"I told you it won't storm tonight," said Donar confidently. "The sky is too clear."

"You don't understand," explained the woman. "It storms every night on Kisalili Island. Asnee calls the lightning and it comes, it doesn't matter what the weather is like."

Even though he felt a warning shiver go through him, Donar knew he had to witness this amazing feat himself. He looked at Ten, and could tell by the expression on his face, that he was intrigued too.

"Where does she call the lightning from?" he asked.

"From Hailstorm Rock," she answered. "At the top of the hill on the other side of Leaf Village. I can draw you a map, but I can't take you there."

"Ok," said Donar.

She picked up a long thick stick from the ground and snapped a twig off of it. Then she drew a map in the dirt.

"I have to go," she said when she had finished. "If you need anything you can find me in the furthest hut from the hill in the Village Green. My name is Spring Green." The woman hesitated. "You won't tell anyone about Plum, will you?"

"Plum?" asked Donar unsure.

"My baby," she explained softly, nodding at her bundle.

"Oh no. We won't say anything," said Donar. But before he could ask why, the woman was hurrying through the trees.

"Thank you," called Donar. Then he turned to Ten. "Are you ready?"

Ten didn't reply, but he smiled as Donar handed him the stick that Spring had taken the twig from. Ten tested its strength by leaning his weight on it. It held.

Donar thought Ten looked more like himself with a walking stick, however, this time it was Ten who followed Donar through the trees.

They passed through the forest that ran between Village Green and Orange Town. It was getting darker now and they didn't meet anyone. Soon they saw the hill rise from the flat land. A huge irregular shaped rock emerged from the top of the hill as if it was trying to get out of the earth. It was three feet tall and at least twenty feet at the widest point. Although most of the hill was covered in long grass or small shrubs, there were three thick trees close together that provided a perfect hiding place for them.

They sat there silently, waiting impatiently with terrified anticipation. Just when Donar feared it would get too dark to see, a shimmering light appeared wavering on the other side of the rock. It was getting closer. Finally he could see that it was actually a woman. She was tall and thin and silver. She wore a tight silver sparkling dress unlike anything Donar had seen before. Her hair and skin were also silver. They glimmered brightly, sending sparks through the air as she walked. Donar was mesmerized with the terrible elegance she portrayed.

When she reached the rock, she threw sparkles across the top of it. There was so much light between the rock and the woman, Donar didn't even realize the sun was completely gone. He held his breath, waiting for something spectacular. He didn't have to wait long.

Asnee raised her arms high in the air and with a piercing sharp voice she said:

Powers of the darkest night,
Who shock and stun and jolt,
Send to me your strongest light,
I need a lightning bolt.

Suddenly the sky was lit with silent lightning strikes. The burst of light was so abrupt and so strong that Donar feared he was blinded. In fact, he couldn't see for several seconds until his eyes adjusted to the dimness again. Asnee continued to chant:

Send your lightning through my arm,
Fill me with your potion,
Let the lightning do it's harm,
To put my plan in motion.

All at once the skies opened and the rain poured down in piercing sheets. The lightning flashed silently and ferociously. Donar and Ten found themselves in the middle of a raging storm, as Asnee's words went on:

Send to me a tender age,
Who can not protest strife,
Turn tranquil quiet into rage,
So I can capture life.

PART FOUR

Excerpt from Elaine's Journal

March 28

I was quite worried when I first found out that Zoe could disappear through a door in Mrs. Nestor's house at any time. Mrs. Nestor felt that Zoe's first birthday would be an especially dangerous day, as it was the day she was born that she received the medicine from Keenan.

I almost wore myself out being at Zoe's side constantly to make sure she was safe. But now it's been a whole week since her birthday and nothing has happened. Finally I am able to relax.

61

Chapter twenty

Hope Town
Ontario
Canada

Elaine was sitting on the kitchen floor showing Zoe all the new toys she had received for her birthday. Zoe was bubbling happily. She was a pretty child with dark brown fly-away hair and deep chocolate eyes. Each toy that Elaine handed her, she grasped tightly, studied intently, tasted carefully and then threw away. She smiled at Elaine and waited for the next item. It was a fun game.

The kettle on the stove started to boil and Elaine's mom hollered from the living room. Elaine stood up and unplugged the kettle, and Zoe's smile disappeared.

"Lay-lay," she cried which was as close as she could get to saying Elaine's name. "Lay-lay," she whimpered and held up her arms.

"Don't worry Zoe. I'm right here," said Elaine as she picked up the little girl and hugged her closely. "I'll always be here for you, no matter what happens," she promised. This time her promise was lighthearted, instead of filled with dread and worry. Since Zoe's birthday had come and gone without incident, Elaine felt much happier. As long as she kept Zoe away from Mrs. Nestor's house, everything would be fine.

Elaine gazed out the window. It was a gorgeous day. The snow had melted and the sun had shone for several days, so the ground wasn't as wet as it should be for early spring. It was a day to be outside, a day that promised summer's warmth. She could hardly wait for her friends to arrive. She was going to suggest a picnic at the treehouse. This time they wouldn't have to shiver while they were eating, and they wouldn't have to listen to Brooke complaining about the cold weather. Elaine loved her treehouse. She would eat there everyday if she could.

Her friends arrived together, and soon everyone was crowding around the kitchen packing up enough food for twenty people.

"Pass the mustard," said Clark, who was in charge of sandwiches.

"Where's the big thermos we always use?" asked Adam with his head inside a cupboard.

"Lay-lay," shouted Zoe trying to get Elaine's attention.

"I'm coming, my favorite little cousin," said Elaine passing the thermos to Adam.

"Seeing as she's your only cousin, there's not much competition," said Clark dryly.

"She would be a favorite even if there were a hundred cousins, because she's so cute," said Brooke, patting Zoe's head.

"Of course she would," smiled Elaine's mom as she and Aunt Meredith sat down at the kitchen table and joined the busy group.

Brooke held Zoe up to the window so she could look outside while the others finished up the picnic. Then they put their jackets on. Zoe whimpered as if she suddenly realized they were going to leave her behind. She lifted her arms to them pleadingly.

"Oh look," said Brooke, "Zoe wants to come with us."

"Aunt Meredith," said Elaine. "Would it be all right if we took Zoe outside with us?"

"I don't know Elaine," said Aunt Meredith. "I'm awfully nervous about her falling out of the treehouse."

"We could have our picnic on the ground," said Brooke

"There's a plastic ground sheet in the treehouse. We could spread it under the blanket to stay dry," added Adam.

"Well, it is a beautiful day," said Aunt Meredith giving in.

"And there are four of them," said Elaine's mom with a smile.

"Ok," said Aunt Meredith, "but please be careful."

"We will," said Elaine happily. What could possibly happen?

Chapter twenty-one

Elaine had to giggle when she watched Adam and Clark hold Zoe's hands to help her slowly walk around. Elaine and Brooke pretended to chase her and Zoe squealed delightedly.

Zoe was fascinated by everything in the forest. She babbled to the chipmunks that were brave enough to be seen. She touched every tree trunk in amazement, running her tiny hands over the rough bark. They had to watch her carefully, because she wanted to taste every leaf and even the dirt.

When Zoe seemed tired out, they sat her on the blanket and opened their picnic. Brooke rooted through Zoe's diaper bag for the snacks Aunt Meredith said they would find there.

They each had their fill and the warm sun was making them lazy. Clark laid down and closed his eyes. Elaine figured he would fall right asleep after all the food he had devoured. Adam opened his journal and began writing something. Brooke pulled a tiny sewing case out of her pocket and opened it carefully. Elaine gave Zoe her bottle and snuggled her close.

"What are you working on Brooke?" Elaine asked.

"Mrs. Nestor gave me this little kit and some fabric to embroider. Your mom said she would help me too. I'm making a pin cushion for my mom's birthday. See?" She showed Elaine the beginning of some colourful flowers embroidered on a small square cloth.

"That's pretty, Brooke. Your mom will love it," said Elaine trying not to yawn. She was feeling drowsy.

Zoe laid down on the blanket with her bottle in an iron grip. She closed her eyes, and Elaine marveled at her long eyelashes, they were so dark against her baby soft skin. Everyone was quiet, and the sun shone on Elaine's face. Maybe she would close her eyes just for a moment. She laid her head beside Zoe. She felt so relaxed. Summer was on its way and there were so many things...

Suddenly Elaine felt ice cold. Something was wrong. Something made her sit up straight. What was it? She looked around desperately and realized Zoe wasn't beside her anymore. Her heart pounded so loudly, she expected the others to hear it and rush to her aid. She placed her hand over her head to shade the sun from her eyes and looked around in a panic. A muffled cry came from her throat as she saw Zoe. She was crawling up the treehouse ramp! By the time Elaine got to her feet, Zoe was teetering near the very top!

Somehow at a time when she should be crying out hysterically, Elaine realized that if she screamed, Zoe could be startled and fall over the edge of the ramp. There were no sides on it to keep her steady. So, with a panic-stricken whisper, Elaine finally got the attention of the others. Everyone jumped up in alarm. Elaine rushed to the ramp. By the time she reached it, Zoe had gone inside the treehouse, which was at least safer.

Just when Elaine felt that maybe her heart wouldn't burst through her skin after all, she reached the treehouse entrance, but when she looked inside, Zoe wasn't there!

Chapter twenty-two

"She's gone!" Elaine screamed freely now, for Zoe wasn't there to be startled anymore. "She's gone! Where did she go? Where could she go?"

Her friends were behind her now. Adam held her steady, while Clark raced around the tiny square room as if Zoe could have hidden in a crack of the wooden walls. Brooke began to sob quietly.

"Adam," Elaine turned to grasp his shoulders. "Where's Zoe? Where is she? What happened?" As they looked deep into each other's eyes, they both remembered the conversation with Mrs. Nestor. Elaine felt that she and Adam were speaking to each other without words, as their thoughts raced in the same direction.

"But we're not at Mrs. Nestor's house," said Elaine quietly to him.

"I don't understand it either," he whispered. "But it's the only possibility." He wrapped his arms around her and held her close as she cried into his shoulder, making a damp spot on his sweatshirt.

Clark and Brooke had run down the ramp and searched around the trees. Now they came back to the treehouse with terrified looks on their faces.

"She's not anywhere on the ground," said Clark in a frightened squeak.

Elaine wiped her eyes. "Of course she's not. We all saw her go into the treehouse."

"We couldn't have," said Brooke anxiously, "or she'd still be there."

"And she's not," whispered Clark almost afraid to say the words out loud.

Elaine started to tremble and Adam took her hand.

"We think she may have gotten to Keenan somehow," Adam explained.

"Why here? Why now?" asked Clark confused.

A strangled cry came from Elaine.

"What is it?" he asked gently.

"Today." It was all Elaine could get out, her voice catching on her sobs.

"Oh," said Brooke suddenly.

"What?" asked Adam.

"Today is the day Zoe was baptised," said Brooke.

"Oh no!" said Clark with his eyes wide. "We were so worried about the medicine from Keenan she received on her birthday, we didn't remember about the water from Keenan that she was baptised with."

"It was a year ago today," cried Brooke, her eyes wide with horror.

Adam glanced at Elaine. He knew she would blame herself for not remembering. He dreaded meeting her eyes, but when he finally looked, she was staring at something on the blanket.

"Brooke," exclaimed Elaine with a screech. "Where's your embroidery?"

"What?" asked Brooke. She couldn't understand why Elaine would care about that now.

"Your piece of fabric from Mrs. Nestor," cried Elaine in despair.

"On no," cried Adam. "Zoe must have taken it. If it was from Mrs. Nestor's house, it could have been a magical connection."

"Is there any more fabric?" asked Elaine frantically.

Brooke didn't understand why Elaine wanted more, but she decided it was not the time to ask. She grabbed the little sewing kit and pulled out another small piece of cloth and handed it to Elaine.

"If this is a magical connection, it should work for us too," said Elaine.

It was a desperate plea and Adam hoped with all his heart that she was right.

"Well, let's try then," said Clark kindly.

"Try what?" whispered Brooke to Clark.

"To go to Keenan after her," he explained softly.

"Wait," said Brooke. She ran down the ramp, grabbed Zoe's diaper bag from the blanket, and ran back up again.

Elaine tucked the piece of cloth into the pocket of her jeans, and joined hands with Brooke and Adam. She looked out the small treehouse window which was the only opening. She peered intently into the forest, but she could only see the familiar trees of her huge backyard.

Then Clark grabbed Brooke's hand, and suddenly they all gasped. For although the sun was shining brightly through the green plastic roof, outside the treehouse window a dark and violent rain poured down. They saw a flash of lightning. Then following Elaine's lead, and holding hands tightly, they jumped through the window and into a raging storm.

PART FIVE

Excerpt from Elaine's Journal

March 29

I can't believe we were so worried about Zoe going to Mrs. Nestor's house. Zoe must have more magic in her than we realized, because she opened a brand new door, and created a passageway to Keenan on her own.

And you won't believe what happened after that...

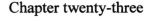

Chapter twenty-three

Kisalili Island
The Land of Keenan

Elaine, Adam, Brooke and Clark stood huddled together. It was extremely difficult to see anything, partly because of the darkness of night, and partly because of the blinding rain.

"Zoe!" screamed Elaine. "Zoe. Where are you?" She ran desperately around in circles even though she knew it was useless.

"Come on," said Adam spying a large fir tree. "Let's wait beneath those branches until the rain slows down."

"I can't leave Zoe!" cried Elaine. "What if she drowns?"

"I've never heard of anyone drowning in a rain storm," said Clark.

"What if she falls in a deep puddle?" screeched Brooke.

Clark just looked at them in horror. For once he was speechless.

They ran around the small clearing crazily. It was impossible to see anything, and finally Adam dragged them beneath the huge fir tree. The lowest branches were almost four feet up the massive trunk, and they drooped to the ground, creating a canopy which was fairly effective in keeping the rain out. Adam was more concerned with hiding under the branches, rather than using them for protection from the rain. They were already completely soaked. He felt uneasy, the little bit of landscape he could see, was completely unfamiliar to him. The four of them gathered together somberly. The tears on Elaine's face mingled with the rain drops.

"What are we going..." began Elaine.

"Shhh," Adam interrupted her. "I hear something."

Unexpectedly, a branch lifted up and a boy's face peered in.

"Can I come in?" he asked politely.

"Of course," said Adam in surprise.

"Thanks," said the boy. "My name is Donar. I saw you climb under the tree." He wasn't sure whether he should also tell them, he saw them jump out of thin air, and run around foolishly in circles.

"Did you see a baby?" asked Elaine. "She's a one-year old with brown hair."

"So that's what she picked up," replied Donar to himself. He frowned deeply.

Elaine grabbed Donar's shoulders. "Who picked her up? Who has her? Where is she?"

Adam pulled Elaine's hands away from the shocked boy. "I'm sorry," he said. "We're looking for her cousin, who's lost and we're all very worried. If you could tell us anything, we'd be grateful."

"Oh," said Donar recovering from Elaine's attack. "I'll help you," he said, "but I'm afraid that Asnee has your cousin. I saw her pick something up and carry it away. It was the right size to be a small child, and the way she was carrying it, well, I guess it was."

"Quick," said Elaine. "Let's go find her right now."

"Wait!" said Donar a little more harshly that he meant to. "We better think this out. If Asnee has your cousin, we can't go storming up to her and demand the baby back."

"Why not?" asked Adam suddenly afraid.

"For one thing, we're likely to get flashed," said Donar gravely.

"What do you mean - flashed?" asked Clark.

"Asnee has the power to turn people to dust just by pointing her finger at them," explained Donar.

Elaine shuddered and Brooke gasped.

"And she has Zoe!" squeaked Elaine.

"Who is this Asnee anyway?" asked Adam.

"She's the ruler of Kisalili Island," replied Donar.

"Kisalili Island!" exclaimed Elaine looking hard at Adam. "You mean we're not even in Keenan?"

"Oh yes," said Donar. "You are in Keenan."

"But there's no island with that name in Keenan," said Clark.

"Are you sure you don't mean Murasaki Island?" asked Adam. "That's where we've always landed before."

"No," said Donar staring at them. "Murasaki's in the east."

Adam shrugged out of his jacket and perched it over his head and shoulders so he could read his journal notes without rain splattering them. He turned to the page where he had carefully drawn the map of Keenan.

"I copied this from the Wizard's own map, the first time we were here," said Adam, "and there's no Kisalili Island."

Donar peered at Adam's map. "Well, it should be right here." He pointed in the sea beside Raimond Island, directly under the Takara Forest of the mainland. "It's the most southern land in Keenan," he explained. "I've seen the Wizard's map too."

Everyone looked confused.

"We're the Human Elements," said Elaine hoping he would have heard of them. "I'm Fire, and this is Water, Earth and Air."

But Donar just looked at them blankly, without saying anything.

Chapter twenty-four

The five of them sat shivering and dripping in the dark forest, talking about what they should do. Elaine reluctantly agreed with Adam that they should hear everything Donar had to say before rushing off to find Asnee. But it was extremely difficult for Elaine to stay still when her beloved Zoe could be getting flashed to pieces.

Donar was worried for them, but he was also happy for himself. Perhaps if he helped them, they would help him. They seemed like they would be that way. He had the feeling they were important even though he had no idea who they were, or how they had mysteriously appeared. They were obviously from another world, and that, in itself, was very exciting.

Donar explained how the Wizard had come to find him and brought him here to stop Asnee from something, but he didn't know exactly what. He told them how they had watched her call the lightning, then how he had sent the Wizard back to their hut to rest because he had been hurt earlier. Then he explained that he had seen them hide under the tree.

"What did Asnee say to call the lightning?" asked Adam curiously.

Donar squinted as he tried to remember the words.

"Something about...sending lightning through her arm to get a potion...doing harm and putting a plan in motion. Then she mumbled about strife and rage, but I remember the last line clearly, because it sounded so strange, it was...so I can capture life."

Elaine cried out at the last line, and Adam reached for her hand. Donar looked at them.

75

Adam explained, "Elaine's cousin is named Zoe, and in our world the name Zoe means life in the Greek language.

"Oh," said Donar in sympathy. So Asnee had captured life. He wondered what that could mean.

Chapter twenty-five

The rain stopped and Donar built a small fire. He hoped that the smoke would drift unseen into the dark sky. They huddled around it, soaking up its warmth and sighing with pleasure when they finally felt dry.

They had decided to sneak up on Asnee and try to find Zoe without Asnee knowing, but nobody was very anxious to go except Elaine who was pacing wildly.

Eventually Donar said they'd better go while it was still dark, so they quickly put out the fire, and set off in the direction Donar had seen Asnee walking.

Once they passed Hailstorm Rock, they quickly spied two buildings. One was a large square stone place with a thick wooden door, the other was a small circular mud hut. They all agreed to spy on the mud hut first, because it wasn't so intimidating. Clark felt that anyone who could flash people to bits would naturally live in a grander home, so he was relieved to start small.

They crept around to the back of the hut, where a small opening had been scooped out of the mud wall. Putting her finger to her lips, Elaine tiptoed over to the tiny window and peered in.

There was a fire in one corner casting flickers of light on the walls of the tiny room. A small woman stood with her back to Elaine, stirring something in a black pot over the fire. She wore a long dress and a scarf over her head. Elaine's eyes searched frantically and sure enough, she saw Zoe curled up on the sleeping platform peacefully. The relief that flowed through her when she saw that her cousin wasn't hurt was tremendous.

Just as Elaine was thinking that the five of them could easily overpower the one woman and take Zoe, she heard the door open and slam against the inside wall. Elaine felt Adam and Donar join her at the window and they looked in awe at the new arrival.

She was a thin woman, so tall she had to stoop in the tiny hut. She had silver skin that glittered horribly, and silver hair that looked as sharp as a knife blade. Elaine glanced quickly at Donar and he nodded. It was Asnee.

Asnee glared at Zoe in the corner and then turned to the little woman at the fire.

'Now remember what I said Crimson," screeched Asnee in a sharp voice. "No harm must come to this child."

Elaine breathed a sigh of relief, then worried it was too loud.

"Yes My Lady," bobbed Crimson.

"I must continue my work and I don't expect to be disturbed in any way," continued Asnee icily.

"Yes My Lady," said Crimson meekly.

Asnee scraped her long silver fingernails into the mud, making lines down the wall. Elaine noticed that Crimson stayed very close to the fire, and that Asnee stayed far away from it.

"It will take me several more days to complete my plans, and then..." Asnee flicked the mud out of her fingernails flinging it onto the clean table in little clumps. "...then I will have the most powerful magic that Keenan has ever seen." She smiled an evil smile.

"What will you do then, My Lady?" asked Crimson bobbing her head respectfully.

"That is none of your concern," sneered Asnee. "For some reason that little lump represents life," she continued to herself. "She must remain my captive."

Suddenly she looked hard at Crimson. "Just remember what I said, and don't let that straggly girl-child out of this hut."

"My Lady, how will I get food and water, if I can't leave?" asked Crimson fearfully.

"That's not my problem. Find help. Just do what you're told... or else." Asnee pointed her finger at Crimson with a snicker.

The poor woman covered her face with her arms. "Yes, My Lady. Yes, My Lady," she trembled. She didn't uncover her head until the twig door had slammed closed and Asnee had left.

Chapter twenty-six

They sat under the fir tree again, out of sight while the sun slowly appeared over the treetops. Elaine suggested that they just walk into the hut and take Zoe while Asnee was busy with her plans. Even if Crimson tried to stop them, they were five against one.

"I know you want to get Zoe and so do I, Elaine," said Adam. "But we have to think ahead. Even if we managed to get her out of the hut, we don't know how to get home."

At this statement, Elaine, Brooke and Clark all gasped. It was true, thought Elaine in despair.

Adam continued, "and since we don't know how to get home, if Asnee caught us, which she probably would, we would all get flashed."

"It seems to me there will be a lot of flashing going on if Asnee gets her way," said Clark gravely.

"That's the other thing," said Adam. "Donar said he and the Wizard came to Kisalili Island to try and stop Asnee from whatever evil she's brewing, and from the sounds of it, they need help."

"I have an idea," said Donar with excitement. He was thrilled that they were thinking of helping him.

"What is it?" asked Elaine.

"If someone went up to Crimson on the pretense of being lost and offered to work for food and shelter, they could take care of Zoe. Crimson needs help, she even said so. Then someone could make sure Zoe was safe and comfortable while the rest of us figure out how to stop Asnee. She said she needs several days to work, so we have until then."

"That's perfect," said Adam. He looked at Elaine.

"It is a good idea," Elaine agreed. "I'll stay with Zoe."

"No," said Brooke firmly.

Everyone looked at Brooke in astonishment. She had hardly spoken until now.

"I'll stay with Zoe," she said.

"Thanks Brooke, but she's my cousin. It's my responsibility," replied Elaine.

"Elaine," said Adam touching her shoulder gently. "I know you want to be with her, but I think Brooke's right."

"What if we need your help?" asked Clark. It was the closest he had ever admitted that Elaine was the leader of their group.

Elaine was surprised at Clark's words, but she didn't give in. "She's my cousin. I made a promise to take care of her."

"I'll stay with Zoe," repeated Brooke with determination. "I'm not good at making plans. I don't know anything about fighting evil, and I can't understand how magic works at all. You all know it's true. Sometimes I don't know why I was included. But there's one things I do know, and that's how to take care of babies." She flung the strap of Zoe's diaper bag over her shoulder as if to emphasize her point. "Maybe that's why I'm here!"

Brooke's speech reminded Elaine of a speech she had made long ago. It was during their first visit to Keenan, when they had learned that the dying magic in the land could be saved, but only if Elaine walked through a fire in a magical ceremony. Even the Wizard was unsure if Elaine would live through it, but she had been determined to save the magic. She felt it was why she had come to Keenan in the first place. Elaine had made a great personal sacrifice, and she knew that Brooke was doing the same thing now, for Brooke's greatest fear was coming true - the fear of being left behind.

"Oh Brooke," cried Elaine. She threw her arms around her friend. "You are a part of us, because we need you, especially in times like this."

"You'll be all alone," said Clark.

"I know," said Brooke. "And I'll be scared."

"But you'll be just fine," said Adam patting her on the back.

"I know Zoe will be safe with you Brooke," said Elaine. The two friends hugged each other tearfully.

A little later, they all watched carefully as Brooke knocked on the door of the mud hut. They held their breath until she went inside. Then they turned and started back to the place where Donar said the Wizard were waiting.

"She'll be all right, Elaine. We even heard Asnee say Zoe wasn't to be harmed," said Adam kindly.

"I hope so," she said in a small voice.

Chapter twenty-seven

It was still too early to see anyone from the three villages Donar had told them about. Although it was morning in Keenan, Elaine's body was telling her she had had a full day. It was only lunch time when they had left home, but they arrived here in the dark and had been wide awake all night. They were tired now.

As Donar lead them through the forest, Elaine wondered about the Wizard. They hadn't really figured out how much time had passed since they were last in Keenan. They did know that the time flowed differently in each world. When they had visited Keenan the second time it was seven months later in their world, but seventy years had passed in Keenan. If Adam's calculations were right and the time in each world flowed consistently, then... Elaine wasn't very good at math and now she used her fingers, tapping them against her leg as they walked. It had been a little over a year since their last visit to get Zoe's medicine, that meant... tap tap tap... about 120 years! Elaine wondered about her old friends, especially Eighteen, the Wizard's apprentice. She found it difficult to believe he was probably gone.

Donar interrupted her thoughts. "We're here," he said happily.

They stared at the tiny mud hut similar to the one Zoe was at. Elaine brushed her hair out of her eyes and prepared to meet the great new Wizard of Keenan.

When Donar opened the door, they saw a very tall man leaning over the fire pit. He wore dirty torn leggings and had blood stained bandages around his bare chest. His hair was messy and he had a day's growth of a beard which made him look shabby.

Elaine, Adam and Clark were shocked. They knew the Wizard had been hurt by a sea dragon but they didn't expect this. Donar felt their discomfort and was a bit embarrassed that Ten hadn't cleaned himself up. But then Ten didn't know Donar would be bringing anyone back with him.

Ten turned around and his face lit up. "Oh Donar! I was afraid something had happened. I didn't expect you to be so long."

Donar was pleased with his concern. "I found some friends to help us," he explained.

"Come in. Come in, and welcome," said Ten. "Although it's not really our hut to welcome you to. We just found it yesterday."

"These are the Human Elements," said Donar to Ten. "This is Fire, Earth and Air."

"Really?" said Ten in astonishment. "Oh my. But, I thought there were four."

"Yes," said Elaine. "Water is at another hut, through the forest." She felt a great relief that he knew about the elements.

"We've been here twice. We met the Seventeenth Wizard and his apprentice Eighteen," added Clark.

Suddenly Ten and Donar stared at each other with a strange troubling look.

"You must be mistaken," said the Wizard kindly.

"Of course, we're not," said Adam.

Elaine didn't speak, she had a very weird feeling.

"Keenan hasn't had a Seventeenth Wizard yet. I am only the Tenth Wizard of Keenan," said Ten.

Elaine, Clark, and Adam looked at each other.

"We've come back in time," announced Elaine in surprise.

Chapter twenty-eight

Elaine awoke from a short nap. She stretched out on the sleeping platform, with a yawn. Then her eyes opened wide with amazement as she remember learning that they had travelled back into Keenan's past. It seems hard to believe. When Elaine had figured that 120 years had passed, it saddened her to think of all her old friends being long gone. Now she had to re-adjust her thinking because they hadn't even been born yet. It felt very strange. She knew what the future held. She imagined herself as a fortune teller with a crystal ball.

Adam and Clark were sitting at the table eating fruit. Adam smiled at her.

"We just woke up too. Donar and Ten went down to the sea to clean Ten's bandages," he said.

"I think Donar's trying to get him looking more... wizardly," said Clark.

"Want some fruit?" asked Adam ignoring Clark's comment and pushing a platter of apples and berries towards Elaine.

"I can't believe we're eating fruit again," complained Clark. "Every time we come to Keenan we starve to death."

"It's better than nothing," said Elaine biting into a juicy red apple.

"Elaine," said Adam, "after you fell asleep, Donar and I went to get some fire wood. We talked for awhile."

"Yes," said Elaine.

"It seems that when Alkuluki..."

"Who?" asked Elaine.

"That's the sea dragon," explained Clark.

"Oh," said Elaine.

Adam continued, "When Alkuluki attacked Donar and Ten they lost all their magical ingredients. They had lilac petals and something Donar calls thinking dust, and it all fell into the sea. They also had the Brown Leather Book which was giving them clues about how to stop Asnee. But now they don't have any magic power to fight her with."

"Did they lose the book too?" asked Elaine.

"Yes," answered Adam glumly. It was a terrible loss. Then he brightened. "But someone must find it, because we've seen it in the future."

"That doesn't help us now, though," said Clark.

"So," said Elaine munching thoughtfully. "What we have to do first is replace the magic. Doesn't this sound familiar?"

Adam and Clark grinned at her.

"This is becoming a habit," agreed Clark, thinking back to their other visits to Keenan.

"I guess Murasaki Island will still have the magic lilacs since they were here before... I mean later. Is that right?" asked Elaine confused.

"It sounds right. But yes, the lilacs are still there because I asked Donar. It's just that Donar and the Wizard don't have any petals to summon Beriah to get to Murasaki Island," explained Adam.

"Wait a minute," said Elaine excitedly. She jumped up and started madly searching the pockets of her jeans. "I wore these pants when we were at Mrs. Nestor's house and I put her lilac filled sachet in my pocket. I noticed there was a little hole in the corner of the fabric." Her hand came out of the pocket holding Brooke's embroidery cloth. She threw it down and dived into the other one. "Which pocket was it in? Oh!" She pulled out her hand and held up one tiny, wrinkled, dried-up, brown, lilac petal.

Adam and Clark looked at her in astonishment.

"Good thing I didn't put them in the wash," said Elaine grinning.

Clark decided not to make a remark about cleanliness. "Surely you don't think that thing will actually summon Beriah?" he asked instead.

"How will we know, unless we try," said Elaine happily. She just knew it would work.

"How will we know what?" asked Donar. He and Ten were standing at the door.

"I found a lilac petal to summon Beriah. Now we can replace the magic," explained Elaine.

Ten's face lit up with joy. "We must get started right away then. We don't have much time. Asnee's power is growing stronger every minute."

"Ten and I will leave immediately and return as soon as we can," said Donar.

"I don't think that's the best plan," said Adam. "I think Donar should stay here. He knows his way around the villages better than we do. We need to keep an eye on Zoe, and we also need to find out what Asnee plans to do, now that the Brown Leather Book is lost. Donar knows more about what's going on than we do."

"That's true," said Elaine.

"I think Ten should have help though," said Donar.

"I'll go with you Ten," said Elaine. "I'd love to see Beriah again."

"No," said Adam. "You need to be here for Zoe. I think Clark should go." He hoped it wasn't too obvious that he wanted to stay with Elaine.

87

Clark didn't really want to go, but when he saw how much Elaine wanted to, he changed his mind.

"Ok," said Clark.

They sat around the table, finalizing their plans, focusing all their hopes on a dismal, little, shriveled-up petal.

Chapter twenty-nine

As much as Elaine wanted to go with the others to the sea to call Beriah, she felt she should check on Zoe. She couldn't believe that Zoe had traveled to another world while she was in her care. She was totally responsible for whatever happened. Elaine hoped with all her heart that she could get Zoe safely back home before Aunt Meredith noticed they were missing. She would not allow herself to imagine her mother's reactions if she went outside to look for them. Aunt Meredith would be hysterical and her mother would be furious. She pushed the terrible thoughts from her mind.

Sadly Elaine said good-bye to her friends and crept silently through the forest to the tiny hut where Brooke and Zoe were. Thankfully Asnee was nowhere in sight, but a dark, thick smoke was hurling out of the chimney of the stone building at a terrible rate. Elaine supposed it was an evil potion and she hoped they would have the magic to fight it.

She peered in the same small window and was startled to see the woman called Crimson only a few feet away. Her name certainly was fitting as she had red hair, several shades darker than Elaine's own. Elaine was surprised to see that her skin was only a bit lighter red than her hair. But it was kind of pretty.

Crimson moved away from the window and Elaine could see Brooke and Zoe playing together on the sleeping platform. They both looked happy. Elaine stared hard, and Brooke feeling her stare, looked around uneasily. Elaine lifted her head a bit higher so Brooke could see her. Brooke smiled when she saw Elaine in the window and she made the OK sign with her fingers.

Elaine smiled, and left, hurrying through the forest, anxious to find out if Ten and Donar had actually summoned Beriah with her tiny petal. She was so distracted, she never saw the green and purple faces peering at her through the leafy bushes.

Chapter thirty

Donar and Adam sat at the table. Their excitement over seeing Ten and Clark ride away over the water, was diminished by their worry. Where was Elaine?

"She should be back by now," said Adam again.

Donar could see the worry in his eyes. He knew there was something special between them.

"She's your girlfriend, isn't she?" asked Donar.

"Yes," said Adam a little too quickly. Well, they had kissed once, he thought..

Suddenly he looked up to see Elaine in the doorway. He smiled in relief and then uneasily wondered what she would think if she had heard what he had said.

Elaine was thrilled to hear that the petal's magic worked. She listened happily to all the details; how they all held their breath as they watched the wilted petal float out into the vast sea all alone, then how everyone cheered when they saw the huge shape of Beriah appear.

"You cheered," said Elaine in horror. "Not too loud, I hope."

"Beriah was still quite far away then," Adam chuckled.

"Yes, we wouldn't dare be loud when he was near," agreed Donar. "What do you think we should do now?" he asked his new friends, hoping they would have an idea.

"Well, I don't know about you two, but I want to know what's behind that curtain on the back wall," announced Elaine.

Adam was surprised. He hadn't even noticed it. Donar noticed it, but he hadn't given it any thought. His mother was always hanging fabric on the wall to dry. But when Elaine pulled the curtain aside, Donar let out a shocked squeal.

Behind the curtain was a small desk. Over the desk, a scroll of paper had been nailed to the wall. On the paper, someone had painted a picture. Donar stared at the picture in disbelief. It was an exact replica of mother's sacred tapestry.

Elaine and Adam stared at the painting of a storm gathering over a field of purple flowers, as Donar told them about his mother's tapestry.

Then Elaine noticed a sealed envelope on the desk. It was brittle and yellowed with age. On the front was written one word - Thunder. Donar turned pale when he saw it. His eyes were so huge with astonishment that Elaine knew he was telling the truth when he managed to croak - I think that's for me. He opened it slowly and unfolded the old pages carefully. Then he read the letter aloud.

Dear Thunder:

I am writing to you from another time. I had dearly hoped to be able to speak with you in person when the time came, but alas, I have known for many years it would be impossible. I will have left Keenan long before you are born.

It may surprise you to know that I have been able to see the future of Keenan, and I am aware that a terrible evil will try to destroy everything good and peaceful during your lifetime. In order to prevent this, the First Wizard of Keenan and I have taken some action to prevent such a tragedy.

Because neither of us would be present during this time, we needed to find someone that was pure of heart and strong in faith, that we could bestow the gift of magic upon. In our search, we found your mother, Jurisa.

I have just come from visiting your mother at Aldred Castle. She is a very shy young girl, unaware of the natural magic that flows through her. Naturally she was shocked with our prophesy that she will one day have a son, who will be given the power to save all of Keenan. However, she reluctantly agreed to name you Thunder, so that the First Wizard and I could devise a magic that only someone with your name could claim. Of course, Thunder is a necessary ingredient when trying to fight Lightning.

I cannot explain anymore in this letter, as at this moment in time, the details have not yet been finalized. However we will send to you, the First Wizard's Brown Leather Book. It will guide you.

With faith in all good things,

Elwin Nestor

Chapter thirty-one

"Elwin Nestor!" stammered Elaine. "That's Mrs. Nestor's husband!"

Adam stared at Elaine in amazement. "Elaine, I am completely confounded by the time flow," said Adam in a daze. "It's not logical. How can anyone understand it? Why did it flow at the same rate, the first two times we were here, and not now?"

"If we had come earlier, we could have met Mr. Nestor!" said Elaine. "Maybe one day we still can."

"It doesn't make sense. How did we come back in time anyway?" asked Adam.

"I have a theory about that," said Elaine. "Perhaps each door opens into a different time. If Mrs. Nestor's house is only one door, then it would make sense that the time would flow consistently. But this time we went through the treehouse, which must be a new door. A new door could enter into a new time."

"Of course! Elaine you're brilliant," said Adam in relief. "That must be right..." suddenly he stopped.

They both looked at Donar. In their surprise at seeing Mr. Nestor's name, they had forgotten him. Donar was trembling, his eyes were wide with fear.

"What's wrong?" asked Elaine gently.

"It's all up to me," he stammered. "I have to stop an evil power. I thought I was just helping Ten. But it's up to me, and the Wizard's book is lost. That's how they were sending help. And it's lost!"

A salty tear fell from his eye and landed on the envelope from Mr. Nestor's letter. Suddenly the envelope was much heavier and wet. He looked down. To his astonishment, he was holding the Brown Leather Book in his hands. He looked at Elaine and Adam, they were even more surprised for they had seen the transformation.

"It was in the sea," whispered Elaine watching the sea water drip from the book onto the dirt floor.

"Now we're getting somewhere," said Adam excitedly. "Let's see what the book says."

Donar opened the book and glanced at the first page. The map that he and Ten had studied was blotted out with sea water. But the first poem was still legible although some of the ink was quite smeared. They read it together.

Hidden in the shadowlands,
lives a self-crowned queen,
ignoring Keenan's basic laws,
and filled with hate unseen.

She's lightning sharp, and lightning fierce,
and quick to strike a heart.
and you must use the opposite,
to bolt her realm apart.

She wants to live forever,
but her only aim is strife.
before destruction is complete,
she first must capture life.

She's lightning quick, and lightning mean,
so what to do - you wonder.
the only way to strike a strike,
is with the sound of Thunder.

The three of them sat around Mr. Nestor's table, for Elaine knew now, that undoubtedly it was his hut.

"If your name is supposed to be Thunder, why are you called Donar?" asked Adam.

"Donar means Thunder in a language from your world. At least that's what Ten told me, but I wonder how my mother knew that," said Donar half to himself.

While Adam and Donar were talking, Elaine examined the book. As she suspected, when she turned the first wet page, there were some fresh new dry pages. She gazed at the new poem handwritten in the old brown ink she was so familiar with.

"Look at this," she said to the boys.

Keenan's strength is always four,
Like the friends who cross the door.
They will help to see you through,
The four main tasks that you must do.

Firstly, you must heal the heart,
Of a Village torn apart.
For segregation takes its toll,
You must make the rainbow whole.

"What does that mean?" asked Adam.

"It must be the village here on Kisalili Island," said Elaine. "Didn't you say the villages had colourful names, Donar? They must be the rainbow."

"I think you're right Elaine," said Donar. "And it's not just the names that are colourful."

Chapter thirty-two

The next morning after a much needed sleep, Elaine, Adam and Donar decided to visit the woman from the village that Donar had spoken to. By now the path through the forest was a familiar route. As they passed Orange Town they saw several villagers, doing their morning chores. Elaine and Adam quietly admired the bright orange skin and hair of the short, stocky people gathering wood and fetching water.

Donar asked a young boy where he could find the woman called Spring Green. The boy looked shocked.

"She's not here. She wouldn't be here. She lives in Village Green. It's through the forest that way."

"Thank you," said Elaine, wondering why the boy looked so upset.

Soon they found Village Green. Donar remembered that she said her hut was the furthest from Hailstorm Rock when Spring drew him the map in the sand. They passed several children as they made their way to the last hut.

"Their hair is as green as yours is red, Elaine," said Adam

"There she is," said Donar as he spotted Spring about to enter her hut.

"Hello Spring," said Donar.

The woman looked surprised and then afraid. She whisked them all into her hut quickly, without even saying hello. When the door was tightly closed, she ran to close the shutter on the window, and only then did she politely welcome them. Her family, who were sitting around the breakfast table, stared so intently at the newcomers that Elaine began to feel uncomfortable.

"Sit down, sit down," said Spring. "Help yourself to breakfast, while I introduce my family."

Donar and Adam, who hadn't eaten anything but fruit lately, spied the big fluffy pancakes and quickly took Spring up on her offer. Adam took a plate for Elaine too, she seemed shy for some reason.

"This is my husband, Hunter Green, my son Forest Green, and my daughter Pine Green," said Spring. "I'm afraid I don't know your names."

Adam quickly introduced them between bites.

"Hey, where's little Plum?" asked Donar.

Instantly the Green Family's mouths dropped and Pine's cup of milk fell from her hand and pooled over the table. Nobody moved to clean it up.

"How do they know?" Hunter asked his wife angrily.

"Who's Plum?" asked Elaine.

"Plum is their little baby," said Donar confused.

"Don't forget to mention that she's purple," said Pine bitterly.

"What difference does it make what colour she is?" asked Elaine. But nobody answered her.

"When we met, Spring thought Ten and I were spies for Asnee. She thought that we were going to take Plum away," Donar told Adam and Elaine.

"Why are you so afraid?" inquired Adam gently.

A baby cried behind a curtain, and Spring sighed. With heavy steps she went to get Plum and brought her to the table.

"She's not my baby," Spring whispered, as her family looked on, stunned at her admission. "She's my sister's baby, but she and her husband were..." Tears came to her eyes and she couldn't continue.

98

"They were flashed by the Lady of Lightning," said Forest angrily.

"Why?" asked Elaine.

Nobody spoke.

"I'll tell you why," said Pine. "Because they were different colours. That's why." She spoke in the quiet tone people use when they are extremely mad. "Plum's mother, Turquoise fell in love with a Red. But that's not allowed. When the Lady of Lightning found out about them, she flashed them. My mother managed to save Plum, but we have to keep her hidden."

"That's horrible," stammered Elaine. "It's so unfair."

"I can't believe it," said Adam in disgust. "What difference does it make what colour your skin or hair is?"

Elaine touched Adam's hand and looked at Donar. "The poem from the Book," she said.

Suddenly they understood. Their first task was to end the devastating unfairness that had separated the villages.

Chapter thirty-three

As Elaine spoke with Spring and Pine, she found out that they had gone to great lengths to keep Plum hidden. If Asnee found out about her, Plum would be sent to Purple Place to live in a village where nobody would love her, and Spring couldn't bear that. Elaine who was thinking about Zoe, understood perfectly. She felt so much better knowing Brooke was with Zoe.

Donar, who was thinking back to the time when he and Ten hid behind the bushes, suddenly realized something.

"I think Pine has a particular reason for her strong hatred of this absurd separation, don't you?" he asked.

Pine looked at him in astonishment, but then she said, "Yes. I'm in love with Tangerine Orange."

Donar smiled as he remembered turning away from the couple to give them privacy.

Hunter, who had been silent, listening fearfully to his family confess deadly secrets, now turned to the three strangers.

"So what are you going to do with this information?" he demanded harshly.

"Oh that's easy," replied Elaine lightly. "We're going to change things."

Nothing she could have said would have surprised the family more.

"How?" Hunter demanded.

"To begin with," said Donar, "the Tenth Wizard of Keenan is collecting his most powerful magic. We expect him back very soon. Also, Adam and Elaine have been sent here from another world to help me destroy the one you call the Lady of Lightning."

"And who are you?" asked Hunter in astonishment.

Elaine answered, "Donar is the most powerful Thunder, whose strength comes from the First Wizard of Keenan, who chose him before he was born to send hope and peace back to the land."

An awed hush came over the hut, even Donar was flabbergasted at her answer.

Finally Forest asked, "Why were you sent here? Do you have similar problems in your world?"

Elaine nodded slowly. "Adam and I come from a world, where problems like this have destroyed people. We are lucky, we haven't experienced it ourselves, we live in a country that has tried very hard to promote equality between all people. But we have heard about cruelty so terrible that I can't bear to even talk about it."

"And it's still going on, in some places in our world," said Adam with great sadness.

Donar looked at them in surprise. Perhaps they would have understood all the signs he had seen since he arrived; the fear, the sadness, the anger. He felt hopeless, but then he remember Elaine's speech about him. He had the power to change this.

"We will end this!" he announced firmly. "The villages will unite, and together we will conquer the evil flashes of Lightning that separate people who belong together," he boomed. He banged his fist on the table, making the dishes rattle, to emphasize his point. "But we will need your help," he added meekly.

"Of course," said Hunter Green, and his family nodded enthusiastically.

Chapter thirty-four

Adam and Elaine decided to check on Zoe while Donar talked to the people in Village Green. As they walked to the small hut behind Hailstorm Rock, Adam decided to try and hold Elaine's hand. Elaine smiled at him and clasped her fingers warmly over his.

"Adam," she said. "I've been thinking about the whole time flow thing."

"Yes," said Adam happily. He couldn't believe they were holding hands.

"When we first came to Keenan, we found out there had been other Elements before us - in the past."

"Yes," said Adam smiling.

"Well, now that we've come back in time, do you think that we could be the Elements that we heard about then - now that we are in the past?" asked Elaine.

"I suppose," said Adam dreamily.

"Imagine if we were the only Elements that have ever visited Keenan, other than the first ones who became the first King and Wizard and the others," said Elaine. "Imagine if it was always us, coming through different doors at different times."

"What!" said Adam stopping suddenly, for he just figured out what Elaine was saying. "Elaine! That's amazing."

"I know," she grinned. "Look. There's Crimson going to the village. Hurry. We can talk to Brooke alone."

They ran to the hut and called Brooke. She came to the door with Zoe in her arms.

"Lay-lay," shouted Zoe in glee. She held out her arms to Elaine.

"Don't come in!" shouted Brooke desperately. "Asnee set up a trap on the hut. If anyone other than Crimson goes in or out, a lightning bolt will flash them. We're trapped," said Brooke tearfully.

"Lay-lay," called Zoe.

"Oh Zoe. I love you," said Elaine. It was killing her not to be able to hold Zoe in her arms.

"How did you get past the trap?" asked Adam.

"She set it up after I got here. I think she was nervous because I wasn't a villager," explained Brooke.

"So I can't even hold her," moaned Elaine looking sadly at her cousin.

"I'm sorry Elaine," said Brooke tenderly.

"Do you need anything?" asked Adam.

"No," said Brooke. "Thank goodness I brought Zoe's diaper bag though. Crimson has been wonderful. She's washed out Zoe's diapers and gone to the village to get milk from somebody's cow. She's very lonely. She's one of only a few Reds left on Kisalili Island, and she's not allowed to talk to anybody in the villages because she's a different colour."

"We know. It's terrible," said Elaine.

"I told her everything," admitted Brooke quietly, fearful of Elaine's reaction.

"That's ok," said Elaine. "Tell her we're working on changing things."

"Come on Elaine," said Adam. "We better go."

"Bye Zoe. Be a good girl for Brooke. We'll be together soon," said Elaine.

"Lay-lay," cried Zoe.

As Elaine turned to walk away from her crying cousin, her heart felt so cold that it was a comfort to have a warm hand to hold.

Chapter thirty-five

Elaine, Adam and Donar met back at Mr. Nestor's hut for lunch. They ate some fruit from the nearby trees, and had some of the bread and cheese which Spring Green had given Donar. While Elaine and Adam were visiting Brooke, Donar had been planning a huge village meeting. Pine, Forest and Hunter were spreading the news, and everyone would gather deep in the forest this afternoon.

Elaine thought that since the first task was in motion, perhaps the Brown Leather Book would have some more instructions. Donar opened the book carefully and nodded to show that Elaine was right. He read the poem to himself first, and then read it aloud to Elaine and Adam.

Keenan's strength is always four,
Like the friends who cross the door.
They will help to see you through,
The four main tasks that you must do.

Firstly you must heal the heart,
Of a Village torn apart.
For segregation takes its toll,
You must make the rainbow whole.

The second task's already done,
Before you realized it was one.
You used your thoughts to change a mind,
To make a cruel creature kind.

104

And now we get to number three,
Remove the evil that you see.
It's up to you to change the sight,
Within a fabric woven tight.

When these three tasks are all complete,
You will face your greatest feat.
Use the magic thinking dust,
Share only with the ones you trust.

Fight your foe within a crowd,
With the boom of thunder - loud.
What you think will now come true,
You know what you have to do.

"Do you know Donar?" asked Elaine.

"What?" asked Donar coming out of a trance.

"Do you know what you have to do?" she asked.

"I think so," he replied.

"What does it mean - you used your thoughts to change a mind?" asked Adam.

Donar told them the whole story of what happened when Alkuluki attacked. He explained how he used Ten's thinking powder to change the vicious sea dragon into a gentle creature. There were so awed at what he had done, he felt kind of embarrassed.

So he explained the way he discovered how the thinking powder worked by thinking a hole in his leggings even bigger than the one he had torn instead of fixing it. They all laughed and Donar felt better.

"What do you think the third task is about?" asked Elaine turning back to the Wizard's book.

"I'm not sure, but I have the feeling it has to do with my mother's tapestry," said Donar.

"I think so too," agreed Elaine looking at the drawing of the storm over Mr. Nestor's desk.

"Do you think that means somebody has to go to Donar's hut in the Takara Forest and get the tapestry?" asked Adam.

"Maybe," said Elaine. She looked at Donar for his opinion.

"I guess so," he agreed, "but we'll have to wait until Ten and Clark return. Maybe we should search Mr. Nestor's hut. There might be some old petals in his desk."

"At this rate there will be nobody left to be a crowd for Donar to be within," said Adam frowning. "I guess I should be the one to go. At least I know where it is."

Donar looked surprised, so Elaine explained that the four of them had traveled through the Takara Forest on their first visit - which was in the future. Donar shook his head, it was just too difficult to imagine. He had been an ordinary boy living an ordinary life with his mother in the forest. Then suddenly he was receiving letters from the past and making friends from the future. He heard Adam making plans with Elaine to go and get the tapestry and he wished it could be him. If only he could run home to his mother and hide in the safety of their tiny hut. But he couldn't go and he knew it. His job was to *think* the evil out of Kisalili Island.

Chapter thirty-six

Donar was overwhelmed at the number of villagers gathered in the forest. It was amazing. He stood at the edge of the group with his mouth open. He had never seen so many people before. Elaine and Adam were behind him. Elaine's hand was on his back gently edging him into the crowd. He felt the same way he had when he first saw Ten in the village near his home, he wished he could slink away like he had back then.

Suddenly Hunter Green spotted them, and he barreled his way through the villagers. He and Forest had set up a small platform from logs so the speaker could be seen over the huge crowd. But when Hunter motioned for Donar to climb up the logs, his face looked so pale and frightened, that Elaine volunteered to go instead. She loved making speeches and had won many awards at school. Donar nodded weakly in relief.

Elaine climbed the stacked logs easily and looked out into the sea of faces. There were mostly Greens, Oranges and Purples, but she could also see a few Reds and Blues. They really did look like the rainbow the poem referred to. As people noticed Elaine standing there, they became quiet and soon the forest went from a chattering buzz to a soft hush.

"We have come together today, because we belong together," began Elaine. "We have come together to end the separation of villages, and to end the force behind the separation, so we can live together without fear, and without sadness."

Several people cheered, but they were interrupted.

"Who says we want to be together?" shouted an Orange boy angrily.

"Yeah," hollered a Purple man. "Why would I want to live with a bunch of stupid Greens!" he pointed rudely to a group nearby.

Everyone waited with expectation to hear what Elaine would say. Donar looked worried, and Hunter and Forest looked angry, but Adam was smiling. If anybody could handle this, Elaine could. He had seen her in action at school when bullies picked on smaller kids.

Elaine looked directly at the Purple who had shouted out. "So you don't want to live with the Greens?" she asked solemnly.

"That's right," he said.

"So don't," she replied. The crowd was astonished.

"I thought you said we should live together," shouted a young Orange man. "That's why I'm here. Now you're changing your mind."

"Who do you want to live with?" Elaine asked the young Orange man.

"My name is Tangerine Orange and I want to marry Pine Green," he replied sadly.

The crowd gasped and stared at him, then turned back to hear what Elaine would say.

"So do it," answered Elaine. "And best wishes to you both."

"But that doesn't make sense," shouted a Purple woman.

"Of course it does," said Elaine. "What I'm trying to tell you, is that you should have the choice to do what you want. Where I come from it's called freedom. If that Purple wants to stay with other Purples - he should be able to. Just as the Orange should be able to be with a Green. Each of you should have the freedom to choose for yourselves, but instead you're letting the Lady of Lightning choose for you."

The crowd nodded in understanding.

"But you must remember," continued Elaine, "that if you want to have the choice, you must also respect the choices of others."

"But we can't stop the Lady of Lightning," yelled a Blue man.

"Which village do you live in?" asked Elaine.

"I'm not allowed in the villages. I live in the forest alone," he replied.

"Is that where you want to live?" asked Elaine.

"No," he replied sadly.

"Then stand up and fight for the choice to live where you want," said Elaine.

"But I can't fight the Lady of Lightning," he said in a shocked voice.

"Nobody can," agreed a Green.

"Not by themselves," said Elaine. "But look how many of us there are. There's only one of her."

"There won't be many of us either," said a Red woman. "They probably won't help." She pointed to the Orange and Purple who didn't want to live with other colours.

Elaine looked back at them. "But fighting Asnee, is as much about their choice as it is yours. You have to understand that when someone tells you what to do, even if you would have done it anyway, the fact that you can't change your mind means they control you."

She saw everyone nodding their heads now, even the ones who had disagreed earlier.

"What can we do?" asked the crowd. "What can we do?"

"If we work together - anything!" said Elaine. "To fight the Lady of Lightning, we need the power of Thunder." She motioned Donar to join her. He climbed up the logs, and standing close to Elaine for support, he explained his plan to the people.

Chapter thirty-seven

It was starting to get dark. Most of the villagers had left the meeting and headed for home. A small group still huddled near the platform talking.

"We should head back soon," said Adam, "before the storm hits."

"Yes," agreed Elaine. Then she spotted a small man, half behind a tree, several yards away. He was staring at Donar with an alarming intensity. Elaine turned to touch Donar's arm and nodded in the direction of the man.

Donar turned and stared, then his face broke out into a huge smile and he ran to the man.

"Orvin, Orvin. What are you doing here?" Donar threw his arms around the man, and the man hugged him back.

It was quite some time before Elaine and Adam found out that he was the storyteller from the village near Donar's home, and Donar's dearest friend. After the introductions were made, the four of them began to walk back to Mr. Nestor's hut.

"My dear boy," said Orvin. "I am so proud of all you have done."

"What do you mean?" asked Donar in surprise.

"What do I mean?" laughed Orvin. "How about learning magic, making plans to destroy evil, and trying to reunite the villagers."

Donar was speechless for a moment. "But how do you know all that?" he finally stammered.

"Oh my small friend, I have always known it. Elwin Nestor chose me to watch over you. I have been your secret guardian," explained Orvin.

Donar suddenly felt sad. He thought Orvin was his friend. He didn't say anything, but Orvin must have understood how he felt.

"I would have been your friend, no matter what," said Orvin putting his hand on Donar's shoulder. "You are an interesting and fun companion. The fact that I was asked to watch over you, only made our friendship more special."

Donar smiled.

"Did you really know Elwin Nestor?" Elaine asked.

"Yes. I met him many, many years ago, at Aldred Castle," said Orvin.

"So you were at the Castle," exclaimed Donar. "That's how you knew all those stories. His stories always seemed so real," he explained to Elaine and Adam. Then he remembered the story about his mother. "Orvin, how is my mother?"

"You must miss her," said Orvin softly.

"Yes," said Donar quietly. "Is she all right?"

"She's just fine," said Orvin with a suspicious grin.

"Hey, maybe Orvin would come back with me to get the tapestry," said Adam.

"Oh, so you need the tapestry now, do you?" asked Orvin.

"You know about that too?" asked Donar.

"Will you come with me then?" pleaded Adam.

"No need to," said Orvin mysteriously.

"What?" said Elaine and Donar together.

"Jurisa's waiting for you at Elwin's hut. She has the tapestry with her."

"My mother's here!" shouted Donar, jumping up and down. "Hurry everyone."

Chapter thirty-eight

As they reached Mr. Nestor's hut, the lightning began to flash furiously in the dark sky. It couldn't dampen the spirits of the reunion between Donar and his mother though, they raced towards each other, sobbing and hugging. Elaine was pleased for them, but she couldn't help longing for her own family to be together again.

Elaine, Adam and Orvin stayed outside the hut to give Donar and his mother some privacy, but soon the rain forced them inside too. Jurisa clasped each of their hands warmly.

"So this is the Earth who has been strong beneath the feet of my son, and the Fire who has kept him blazing," said Jurisa.

"Hello," said Elaine pleased. She liked Jurisa at once.

They sat around Mr. Nestor's table, and Donar told his mother and Orvin the plan for destroying Asnee. Jurisa had a worried expression, but was silent. Orvin agreed it was the only way.

"Judging from the strength of that last flash, we don't have much time left," Orvin stated as he watched the lightning through the tiny window.

Everyone peered through the window silently.

"Mother, how did you know we needed the tapestry?" asked Donar. He didn't want to talk about the plans with Asnee anymore.

She looked lovingly at her son. "Just as Orvin was your guardian, I have been the Keeper of the Cloth."

"The name Jurisa means storm in Elwin's world," explained Orvin. "Who better to guard the tapestry

113

portraying a storm, and have a son named Thunder."

"Why didn't you tell me, Mother?" asked Donar.

"Many reasons," she answered. "But, those who are faced with an enormous task, are often too important to learn the very skills that will ensure their success."

While everyone was contemplating this, Jurisa brought out the tapestry and unrolled it on the table.

Elaine gasped at the beauty of it. If only her mother could see this. It was truly a work of art.

"What do we have to do?" asked Donar.

"I am the Keeper and I have kept it. That is all," replied Jurisa.

"I don't know either," said Orvin. "What does the Brown Book say?"

Adam got the book from Mr. Nestor's desk and read the stanza:

And now we get to number three,
Remove the evil that you see.
It's up to you to change the sight,
Within a fabric woven tight.

Elaine who had been studying the tapestry closely, wishing she could tell her mother about it, ran her hand across the smooth fibers. Her hand felt the raised section of threads, that her eyes had missed. She peered down at the stitches. The lightning bolts were not woven into the tapestry, but stitched over top, as if they had been added later.

"I think I know what we have to do," Elaine announced. "Remove the evil that you see, must refer to those lightning bolts. We need to un-pick those stitches."

Jurisa looked horrified. "You'll unravel the whole tapestry."

"No," said Elaine. "Look how the stitches have been worked over top of the rest of the tapestry. If we're careful, you'll never know anything has been removed."

Jurisa examined the tapestry carefully. "You're right. However did you know?"

"My mother does a lot of needlework," explained Elaine.

"A lot - doesn't quite cover it, actually," said Adam punching Elaine's arm playfully.

The boys made a fire, to fight the cold night air, and provide the light for Elaine and Jurisa, as they carefully worked to remove the evil silver thread. Their comfortable silence made a cozy scene, and when the door of the hut was flung open, everyone was startled. Elaine and Adam weren't sure who the very grand man with the purple satin cape was, at first. Then Clark poked his head around the door and they realized it was the Wizard.

"You're back," shouted Donar happily. Then he looked grave. "Tomorrow, we put our plan into action," he whispered fearfully.

Chapter thirty-nine

The next morning, a small group walked solemnly to the hut, where Brooke and Zoe were. Elaine looked nervously at the large stone building, where foul smoke was still bellowing out of the chimney. Elaine went to the back window of the little hut and called Brooke and Crimson. She warned them what was about to happen. She glanced lovingly at little Zoe, but then hurried to join the others.

The villagers were coming to the meeting area slowly and fearfully. Donar, Adam and Clark had been up early spreading the news that the Wizard was back. Ten, Orvin and Jurisa were speaking carefully with each villager, trying to assess their true intentions before giving them a small pinch of magical thinking dust. The villagers held it reverently, and joined the rest of the group with great seriousness. They knew that the dust only worked for Wizards and that only the strength of Thunder gave them the temporary power of a Wizard's magic.

Finally Ten went to join Donar and handed him a pouch of the remaining dust. Elaine could hear Donar's rapid breathing, she wished she could say something to him, but he started walking toward the stone building, and it was too late.

Donar rubbed a pinch of thinking dust onto the walking stick Ten had given him. Then he held the stick high in the air. He thought as hard as he could - of thunder. Suddenly a crackle of thunder filled the air. It was so loud, several people let out a scream. Donar waited. Each second seemed like an eternity. Then all at once the door of the stone building flew off its hinges with a flash. Asnee stood in the doorway. Her silver skin glistened sickly, and her silver hair glinted so brightly, Donar wished he could close his eyes.

"Who dares to interrupt me?" she screeched.

"It's time for you to leave," said Donar in a calm voice. He was amazed how cool he sounded, even though his knees were trembling.

"How dare you," howled Asnee. She pointed her finger at him. The crowd yelped. Asnee looked at the crowd in surprise, she had only just noticed them. But she didn't stop the lightning from flashing from her finger.

Donar was ready. He threw a pinch of dust at the flash of light. He thought of thunder. A horrendous boom echoed his thoughts, and he watched in amazement as the flash from Asnee's finger floated down harmlessly.

Asnee let out a strangled cry. Nobody had ever escaped her flash before. In her anger, flashes charged out of her fingertips aimlessly, and several bushes caught fire. The crowd backed up.

Adam watched in amazement as Donar and Asnee faced each other. Just like two gunmen in an old Western movie he had watched, they both drew their weapons at the same time. Lightning flashed and Thunder roared, blinding and deafening everyone.

Asnee shot sparks from her right hand into the air. They flew over the heads of the people and flashed a hole in the side of the small hut. Elaine screamed in horror. Smoke filled the air, and Brooke carrying Zoe with a blanket over her head flew from the hole and into the forest.

"Come back," screeched Asnee. "I need that girl-child. I need life. You stupid little human, you're ruining my plans."

Elaine watched in relief as Brooke disappeared, and Crimson hurried after her. She knew Asnee wouldn't try to kill Zoe with a flash, because she needed her for something. Elaine was so intent on watching her cousin escape that she didn't see the flashed from Asnee's left hand fly in her direction. The lightning flashed, just missing Elaine narrowly. But the sparks that shot out as the flash hit the ground, showered around Elaine. The sparks caught her jacket and burst into flames. Suddenly Elaine was covered in silver fire.

Chapter forty

Adam watched Elaine in absolute horror. He tried desperately to get to her, but the crowd was too thick. His stomach wrenched with terror.

By now Asnee realized she couldn't fight Donar whose eyes followed her every move with his own magic ready at hand, so she sent her lightning flashes into the air and scattered them on the crowd. The villagers became hysterical, trying to avoid the searing heat of flashes.

Ten watched in fright as the villagers used their precious magic dust to think out the flames that landed around them.

"Save your dust," shouted Ten frantically. But nobody was listening. They couldn't hear him anyway, Donar's thunder was crashing and roaring all around them.

Ten watched Adam race over to Elaine, and use his dust to think out the flames that covered her. Although he understood, he was terribly worried. Would they have enough dust left, when the time came?

Then suddenly one of Asnee's flashes was sent flying backwards with the magic force of Donar's walking stick. A silver flame landed on the stone building and the foul smoke coming from the building started to hiss. Instantly a terrible explosion lifted the building, and the stones scattered, sailing through the air. People screamed, and pushed and shoved each other in desperation. The large stones slammed into people, and they slumped to the ground. Donar was spared and he quickly noticed Asnee was on the ground too, knocked out by a stone from her own building.

"Now!" screamed Donar.

He raced over to the evil woman and poured the remaining dust on her. He looked up to see his mother, Ten, Orvin and Clark, who was dragging Adam away from Elaine. He didn't have time to think about Elaine now. This was his only chance.

"Help me," he begged. "Think her into a world where she can't hurt anyone," said Donar forcefully.

They all thought, but nothing happened. Then Asnee began to stir and a tiny flash shot out of her finger, burning a hole in Adam's jacket.

"We need more help," screamed Donar in fright.

They yelled frantically, and slowly the villager who were able to, came over. They touched Asnee or touched someone who was already touching her.

"Think," hollered Donar. "Think her into a world where she can't hurt anyone."

Asnee squirmed beneath their grasp. The sky filled with lightning and Donar lifted his walking stick automatically. Thunder roared, and the ground shook violently. They heard a tremendous crack. Hailstorm rock had split completely in two. Then the ground opened up and swallowed half the rock. Donar watched in horror as the earth pulled itself in different directions. When he looked back, Asnee was gone.

Donar slumped in utter exhaustion. Then he heard Adam scream, and he watched in dismay as he raced over to Elaine and pulled the stones off her body. Ten and Jurisa raced over to help him. Ten poured thinking dust over her, but Donar wondered if even magic could help her now.

Chapter forty-one

Adam had insisted on carrying Elaine into the forest himself. They had to get her away from the smoke and the fires that were still burning. He lowered her carefully onto a bed of pine needles, and covered her with his jacket. She still hadn't come around.

Jurisa, Orvin and Ten were tending to the wounded villagers, thinking them well again. Clark and Donar were looking for Brooke and Zoe.

Adam sat holding Elaine's limp hand. He had never felt so helpless. Even seeing Brooke and Zoe hurrying through the trees didn't seem to matter. All he could think about was Elaine. He hardly noticed when they crowded around him.

"Do you think she'll be all right?" asked Donar in a whisper.

"Of course," Adam replied, but the tears in his eyes contradicted his answer.

"Elaine's very strong," said Brooke. A tear trickled down her cheek and landed on Zoe's hair. They all looked at the sleeping baby in Brooke's arms.

"At least we saved Zoe," whispered Adam in a strangled voice.

"Of course we did. We're the Human Elements," mumbled Elaine groggily.

"Elaine," said Adam in delight. "Are you all right?"

"Yes," said Elaine. She tried to get up, but she fell back down.

"Help me up, Adam," asked Elaine.

"Elaine, I think you should just rest. You were covered in flames..." said Adam.

121

"Oh, that was nothing," laughed Elaine. "After all, I am the Fire Element. I think it was the stones that did me in."

She looked at Adam in such a typical Elaine kind of way, that he couldn't help laughing. He put his arms around her fiercely and held her close.

Ten, Orvin and Jurisa hurried over to them, pleased at Elaine's recovery.

"We think you four should return home with your baby now," said Ten with a worried expression.

Just then the ground trembled again and several trees came crashing down.

"What's happening?" asked Elaine.

"Kisalili Island is slowly sinking," said Ten. "The strength of the magic fighting against itself has destroyed the land."

"Oh no," exclaimed Brooke in fright.

"Don't worry," said Ten patting Brooke's arm. "It will take some time for the island to completely disappear."

"What about the villagers?" asked Adam.

Orvin smiled at them. "They're preparing to leave as we speak. There's an island nearby - a bigger one, where they can make a new home."

"A home together, as one village, thanks to your help," said Donar putting his hands on Elaine and Adam's shoulders.

"You mean Raimond Island?" asked Elaine.

"Yes, Raimond Island," said Ten.

"Will they get there in time, before the island sinks?" asked Clark.

"Yes," said Elaine. "And they'll call their new village Thorpe."

Everyone looked at her in astonishment.

"How do you know?" asked Donar.

"From the map," explained Elaine. "The map we have in the future, doesn't have a Kisalili Island - because it sank. But it does have a village called Thorpe on Raimond Island."

"And Thorpe means small village. I looked it up once," said Adam.

The Tenth Wizard of Keenan looked at the visitors from another world and he boomed with laughter. "Should I tell the villagers that Thorpe is a good name, or should I let them come up with it themselves," he asked.

"I don't know," said Elaine confused. "Do they call their village Thorpe, because I told you the name? That can't be right because I saw it on the map, so it already had that name. It's a circle."

"It is complicated," agreed Donar with a wrinkled forehead.

The ground trembled again, and the earth began to crumble into the huge crevice that divided the land.

"As much as I hate for you to leave, I guess we'd better hurry," said Donar looking at his friends sadly.

"But Donar, we don't know how to get home," said Elaine.

Donar laughed. "You really haven't figured it out yet? And I thought you were only staying to help me. All you have to do is use the thinking dust and *think* your way home."

"Will it really work?" asked Adam.

"Of course," agreed Ten. "We'll help you."

Everyone hugged and said good-bye while the ground continued to shake. As Orvin hugged Elaine, he slipped an envelope into her pocket. She was about to look at it, when Brooke passed Zoe to her. Zoe woke up shouting "Lay-lay" and threw her arms around Elaine in delight. Elaine hugged her cousin tightly. Then Adam sprinkled the dust, and they all thought of Elaine's treehouse.

PART SIX

Excerpt from Elaine's Journal

March 30

Today we are going to see Mrs. Nestor. I can't wait to tell her what happened. Now that Zoe is home safe, the adventure is more etciting. Mrs. Nestor will be shocked when she hears about a new doorway to Keenan.

I'm also looking forward to telling her about the possibility of travelling into the past. It makes me wonder...

Chapter forty-two

Elaine laid back on the blanket at the bottom of the treehouse. She felt so drowsy.

The sun was so warm and comforting, but she felt as if there was something she should be remembering. Hadn't something happened? She squinted out of one eye. The trees were waving under the bright sun. She could see the green plastic roof of her treehouse out of the corner of her eye. Elaine felt Zoe stirring beside her, and she struggled to remember something. Something that had to do with Zoe. She felt Zoe crawling away. That's what it was! Zoe was going to crawl up the treehouse ramp, and if she got to the top, she would crawl through the window and get lost in Keenan. What?!?

Elaine sat up and grabbed Zoe close. She held the squirming baby tightly as her mind raced to understand what she was thinking. How could she know that was going to happen? Suddenly it came back to her. It had happened!

She looked over at Adam. He was sitting up, starring at her in bewilderment. She watched his eyes change slowly to understanding.

"We came back home to the time before we actually left," said Elaine in surprise. She held Zoe firmly. "If I let Zoe go now, and she climbed through the window, would everything happen exactly the same again?"

"I don't know," replied Adam in confusion. "Could we keep going back over and over, and never get out of that time?"

"In another minute, we'll be past the time Zoe left. Will she be safe then?" asked Elaine.

"It makes my head hurt to try and understand it," moaned Adam.

"When we went through the treehouse, we went back in time in Keenan," said Elaine trying to sort it out.

"And when we returned home, we went back in time too," he said helping her.

"Back to before we left," she added.

"So technically, if we never left, then nobody missed us," said Adam with relief.

Brooke and Clark were starting to wake-up.

"Come on," said Elaine. "Let's take Zoe home."

Chapter forty-three

It was a great relief to hand Zoe back to Aunt Meredith.

"My goodness Elaine. Look how filthy you are," exclaimed her mother. "What were you doing out there, rolling in the mud?"

Adam hid a smile as Elaine searched for something to say. She couldn't exactly say she'd been wearing the same clothes for three days, and she'd been through several storms and a fire.

"In fact, you all look grubby," said Elaine's mother turning on Adam. "Why, Adam, you've torn your jacket. It's all stained too."

That wiped the grin off his face thought Elaine smugly.

Aunt Meredith gave Zoe a hug. "Why is there sand in her hair?" she asked fretfully.

"Sand," exclaimed Elaine's mother. "Where ever would they find sand?"

"It's not sand, Mom. It's dirt," explained Elaine carefully.

"Dirt," said Mrs. Maddock in horror.

"And Zoe's diaper is full too," said Aunt Meredith unhappily. "Where's the diaper bag?"

Elaine and Brooke looked at each other in shock. Brooke had left the diaper bag in the small hut when she had run out of the burning hole with Zoe.

"What diaper bag?" asked Adam trying to be helpful. "I don't remember taking a bag outside."

Aunt Meredith glared at them. "Of course you took it out, it's not here. Where is it?"

"I don't remember," said Brooke meekly.

"It was only an hour ago," exclaimed Mrs. Maddock in exasperation.

"And Zoe definitely needs to be changed," Aunt Meredith frowned at them. "I'm surprised you let Zoe sit in this mess, Elaine."

"I'm very surprised at all of you," said Elaine's mother. "I'm afraid you won't be able to look after Zoe again until you show more responsibility," she announced with great disappointment.

Adam thought of all they done to rescue Zoe and he felt sorry for Elaine. It seemed so unfair. But Elaine only smiled weakly in relief.

"Yes Mom," she replied. She had had quite enough of responsibility for now.

Chapter forty-four

Later when Elaine remembered the envelope from Orvin, she pulled it from her pocket. To her surprise it was addressed to Mrs. Ella Nestor.

The next day, Elaine, Adam, Brooke and Clark sat in Mrs. Nestor's tiny parlour.

They told Mrs. Nestor how Zoe had opened a new passageway to Keenan through the window of Elaine's treehouse. Mrs. Nestor sat stiffly with her hand over her mouth in astonishment. Then Elaine handed her the envelope. She gave a startled cry when she saw it.

"It's my Elwin's handwriting," she squealed. "Did you see him?"

"No," said Elaine softly. "But our friend received a letter from him, that he'd written long ago."

Mrs. Nestor nodded and Elaine could see her hand was trembling.

"I think we'll go make some tea for you, Mrs. Nestor. Come on," Elaine ordered the others.

The four of them sat at the little kitchen table. They were so close their knees touched under the gingham cloth.

"I wonder if we could actually find Mr. Nestor, if we went back in time again?" Elaine pondered.

"I was wondering the same thing," said Adam smiling at her.

"Imagine if we could take Mrs. Nestor with us to Keenan. Then she could be with him again," said Brooke dreamily.

That was the first time Brooke ever mentioned going to Keenan willingly, thought Elaine in surprise. She must be getting more adventurous.

"It's probably not possible to take Mrs. Nestor with us. If she could go, why wouldn't she have gone with her husband?" asked Clark, crushing their dreams.

Finally Mrs. Nestor appeared.

"Thank you, my dears. It was a wonderful surprise to receive a letter from my Elwin after all this time." The tears glistened in her bright eyes.

"Was it a good letter?" asked Elaine. It was hard not to pry.

"Yes," said Mrs. Nestor. "And my goodness, there's a lot, I'd like to hear about. But first, Elwin asked me to give you a present."

"He did?" the children exclaimed.

"Yes," she said. "A long time ago, Elwin asked me to make him a needlework picture. He took it to Keenan with him for awhile, and then he brought it back home again. I had forgotten all about it, but he's asked me to give it to you. I'll go get it now."

When Mrs. Nestor returned, she rolled out the canvas, and there, to the surprise of the children, was the tapestry. The purple flowers still sparkled brilliantly, and the dark storm was still brewing overhead.

"You made this?" asked Elaine in amazement.

"Yes," said Mrs. Nestor. "A very long time ago. But that's strange," she mumbled, peering closely at the tapestry. "I was almost positive there used to be lightning bolts on it. In fact, if I remember correctly, Elwin asked me to add them after the tapestry was all finished."

"Yes, he did," said Elaine. And she told the story.

131

EPILOGUE

Excerpt from Elaine's Journal

September 22

Adam, Clark, Brooke and I have had a lot of time to think about our latest adventure. We are all fascinated by the fact that my treehouse is now a doorway to Keenan.

The big question is — will it ever work again?

The Wizard's Cave
Murasaki Island
The Land of Keenan

Donar sat on a square stone, deep in the cave under the tall gray mountain of Murasaki Island. Ten had told him to *think* up something grand to wear, but Donar decided to wear his old gray leggings and his pale gray tunic. The ones that Ten had first given him months ago. He *thought* up a dark green cape to complete his attire, then he polished his boots the old fashioned way (without magic) because it gave him something to do while he was waiting for Ten.

Ten emerged from his private cave wearing a deep purple tunic and a shiny new purple satin cape.

"Donar, you should have chosen something more regal, after all we're going to see King Truman at Aldred Castle today," said Ten as he fastened the gold clasp of his cape.

"I know, but I feel more comfortable in these clothes," replied Donar truthfully.

They walked through the cave together, passing the pool of water, and the flickering purple lights. Ten leaned heavily on his ornately carved walking stick as they made their way through the tunnel and out into the sunshine.

They paused at the cave's entrance. Donar could just see the tops of two huts, deep in the forest of purple flowers. He kicked some pebbles impatiently, as he waited for his mother and Orvin to arrive.

Jurisa looked beautiful in a long golden gown, and Orvin wore a new navy blue cape. They swarmed up to him excitedly.

"Are you ready to officially become the Eleventh Wizard of Keenan?" asked Orvin enthusiastically.

"Not really," answered Donar.

"Why not?" asked Orvin.

"I really don't know enough to become a Wizard," said Donar.

"Which is exactly why you'll be perfect," said Ten with a laugh.

Donar looked at him, puzzled.

His mother smiled and put her hand on his shoulder. "It is those who realize there is always more to learn, who tread carefully, and who strive to seek more knowledge."

"Come on Eleven," said Ten. "The King is waiting. Let's go call Beriah."

Don't miss these exciting adventure of The Keenan Chronicles

To order books in the Keenan Chronicles,
please contact:

ASHLIN BOOKS

558 Upper Gage, Suite 253
Hamilton, Ontario L8V 4J6
Canada
Phone (905) 574-5352
Fax   (905) 383-3200

Book One	Fire, Water, Earth and Air	$10.00
Book Two	Sun, Wind, Rain and Snow	$10.00
Book Three	Thunder and Lightning	$10.00

Plus Shipping

Signed by the Author upon request.

Makes a great gift.

The Wizard was deeply troubled that he didn't fully understand what he was supposed to do. He wondered why the book couldn't explain more to him. Then as he continued to think, he vaguely remembered a conversation he had had years ago between King Truman and one of his friends from another world.

The Wizard studied the hand-drawn map in the book closely. He wasn't sure how far into the forest he would find the Thundercloud, or if his idea was even right.

He hoped, so, he definitely needed help, if it was up to him to fight the evil that threatened the land of Keenan.

For my daughters:

Ashley, who created Kisalili Island.
Lindsey, who created Alkuluki Sea Dragon.

Keep imagining.

Special thanks to all my readers, especially those who have taken the time to write. And for all those who have been waiting for more adventures in Keenan - this one is for you.

Also for their professional help:

Laurie Mahy - cover production and manuscript evaluation.
Marja Taussi - cover design
Krys Brodnicki - manuscript evaluation.
Margaret Evenden - manuscript evaluation.